SUGAR AND SAWDUST

Lady Heartswell

Centuria Books LLC

CONTENTS

Chapter One

CHECK ENGINE LIGHT

The cold in the inherited bakery didn't just bite; it gnawed right through my thin sweater and settled deep into my bones. I stared up at the water stain spreading across the sagging ceiling like a dark, mocking bruise. *Please don't cave in.* I gripped the edges of the flour-dusted countertop until my knuckles turned white. My entire life—every dime I'd scraped together, every bridge I'd burned in the city—was tied up in this crumbling mountain-town ruin. I was supposed to be a pastry chef, not a miracle worker.

I wanted to fill this space with the scent of browned butter, warm vanilla, and caramelized sugar. I desperately wanted to prove I could build something beautiful all on my own, just like I always had. But the crushing weight of the groaning pipes, the shattered front door, and the impossible mountain of labor was choking me.

What if I couldn't carry it this time? For the first time in my fiercely independent life, a terrifying thought crept in: *I can't do this alone.* I squeezed my eyes shut against the prickle of exhausted tears. I just needed one break. One sign that I wasn't going to drown under the debris.

The contractor I hired over the phone back in Seattle took my entire deposit and completely vanished. My bank account currently held exactly three hundred and forty dollars. The grand opening was scheduled in one month. Right now, I didn't even have a functioning toilet.

Wind howled through the broken front window, scattering dead mountain-pine needles across the warped hardwood. The air smelled of wet rot and decades of neglect. This place was called Sugar and Sawdust in my head. Right now, it was just sawdust. And ice. The commercial ovens I ordered were scheduled to arrive soon. If I didn't have the structural integrity of this place secured by then, the delivery men would leave them in the snowdrifts out front.

I grabbed my metal scraper from my canvas tool bag. I attacked the ancient, sticky grime coating the display case glass. My breathing came in short, white plumes of frost. Every scrape of the metal echoed in the vast, empty room. My shoulders burned. I wiped the glass down with a freezing rag. It looked worse than when I started.

Then, a sound cut through the noise of the mountain wind.

High. Thin. Desperate.

A frantic wailing from beneath the floor.

I dropped the scraper. It clattered loudly against the tile. I moved toward the front window, stepping over piles of shattered glass and debris. The floorboards here dipped dangerously. The wood was black with old water damage.

A tiny paw scratched against the underside of the oak planks.

"Hey." I knelt on the cracked boards. "Are you stuck?"

Another miserable, freezing mewl answered me. A stray kitten. Trapped in the crawl-space, right where the icy draft funneled through the cracked stone foundation. The temperature was dropping fast. The sun dipped lower behind the jagged peaks outside. If that animal stayed down there tonight, it would freeze solid.

I fell fully to my knees. The impact sent a sharp shock of pain up my shins. I jammed my bare fingers into the tight crack between the two most rotted boards. The wood was swollen with moisture and frozen tight.

I pulled upward. My muscles strained. The board refused to budge.

The kitten cried louder, a ragged, terrified screech that twisted my gut into tight knots.

"I'm getting you out." I pressed my face close to the floor. "Just hold on."

I wedged my fingers deeper. The rough, splintered edge of the old oak bit deeply into my skin. I dug my heels into the floor and threw my entire body weight backward. The wood gave a sick crack. Sharp splinters sliced straight through my cuticles. Hot blood welled up instantly, slipping down my palms and staining the dark wood. I ignored the stinging pain. I yanked again. The board lifted a quarter of an inch, then jammed completely against a rusted nail.

I let out a harsh cry, my chest heaving. The mountain cold ripped away my strength. I dug my bloody nails into the gap one more time, preparing to tear the wood apart with pure adrenaline.

Then came the heavy crunch of boots on the snow-dusted porch.

The shattered front door groaned backward on rusted hinges. Bootsteps, heavy and deliberate, thudded against the hardwood. The sound was not frantic. It was the slow, measured pace of a man who owned the ground he walked on. A massive shadow stretched across the dusty floor, completely swallowing the weak afternoon light.

I scrambled to look over my shoulder, my bleeding hands still wedged in the floorboards.

The man taking up the entire doorway was a mountain. He wore a heavy, faded flannel shirt that stretched dangerously tight across a chest completely devoid of softness. Broad, impossible shoulders tapered down into a thick waist. The sleeves of his flannel were shoved up past his elbows, revealing thick, ropey forearms corded with heavy muscle and dusted with dark hair. Dirt, grease, and sawdust deeply stained the heavy, dark denim hugging his thick thighs.

My mouth went completely dry. A hot, heavy flush washed over my skin, completely chasing away the freezing air. He wore a thick leather toolbelt slung low over his hips, drawing my gaze directly to the heavy steel hammer resting against his thigh. The leather loops hugged the sharp V of his pelvis. Every inch of him vibrated with raw, unadulterated strength. His hands hung at his sides. They were huge. Thick fingers, heavily calloused palms, knuckles dusted with pale silver scars from years of brutal physical labor. His jaw was square and covered in dark, rough stubble. His dark hair was thick and messy, dusting the heavy canvas collar of his jacket. He was terrifying. He was the most intensely attractive man I had ever seen.

He marched across the room. He didn't ask what I was doing. He didn't introduce himself.

He stopped right in front of me. His massive, steel-toed boots planted firmly on either side of the broken floorboard. I had to crane my neck aggressively just to see his face.

"Move." The single word rolled out of his chest, deep and rough, vibrating straight through the floor and into my bones.

I scrambled backward, entirely overwhelmed by his proximity. I hit the edge of the display counter and stayed there.

He dropped into a crouch. The thick denim tightened over the massive muscles of his thighs. He didn't look at me. He looked perfectly at the cracked floorboard. He reached down with his huge, scarred hands. He wrapped his thick fingers around the splintered oak where I had just been bleeding.

He didn't strain. He didn't brace himself.

His broad shoulders rolled backward exactly once. The thick muscles of his back flexed beneath the heavy flannel.

Crack.

The stubborn, inch-thick oak board snapped clean in half like a dry twig. He tossed the ruined wood over his shoulder. It hit the wall with a loud thud.

He reached his massive hand down into the dark, freezing gap.

A second later, he pulled his hand back. A tiny, shivering ball of orange fur rested in his massive palm. The stray kitten was so small it didn't even cover his fingers. It wailed, a pathetic, high-pitched screech.

The giant's face instantly shifted. The harsh, severe lines of his jaw completely softened. He pulled the tiny animal directly to his broad chest. He unzipped the top of his heavy canvas jacket and tucked the kitten inside, right against his warm flannel shirt.

His huge, grease-stained thumb reached down. He stroked the top of the tiny kitten's head. The contrast was staggering—this brutal, scarred hand moving with impossible, fluid gentleness. He rubbed the soft spot behind the kitten's ears. The wailing stopped immediately. The kitten let out a tiny purr, burrowing its freezing nose into the heat of his massive chest.

My throat tightened. I stared at him, completely captivated. He had destroyed the obstacle in a single second, entirely to offer comfort to a helpless creature.

Then, he zipped his jacket halfway to secure the kitten. He stood up to his full, towering height.

The tender caretaker vanished instantly.

His demeanor flipped with terrifying speed. He turned his fierce, harsh focus directly onto me. A dark scowl carved deep lines into his face. A muscle feathered in his sharp jaw. His dark stare pinned me in place.

"What the hell are you doing?" His voice cracked like a whip in the empty room.

I flinched back. "I was getting the kitten—"

"Step back from the load-bearing wall before you get hurt. Now."

He pointed a thick, heavily scarred finger at the sagging archway directly above where I had just been kneeling. The cracked plaster groaned audibly under the heavy weight of the roof snow.

I pressed my spine harder against the display case. "I wasn't going to let it freeze."

"You were going to pry up a structural floorboard with your bare hands directly beneath a failing header beam?" He closed the distance between us in two long, predatory strides. He stopped exactly six inches away. The absolute width of his chest completely blocked the faint light from the window. The scent of fresh sawdust, cold snow, and clean, masculine sweat rolled off him in a dizzying wave.

He reached out. Before I could pull away, his massive fingers wrapped around my wrists. The heat radiating off his skin burned straight through my freezing limbs. He lifted my hands, inspecting my torn cuticles and bleeding palms. His grip was an immovable vice. Not painful, but completely inescapable.

His jaw clenched tighter. The muscle jumped again beneath his skin. "You're bleeding."

"It's just a splinter." I tried to pull my hands back.

He didn't let go. His rough thumbs brushed over my torn skin, a calloused, rasping friction that sent a hot jolt straight up my arms. Gooseflesh rose rapidly over my skin. "You don't know the first thing about this building. The foundation is compromised. The plumbing froze solid three days ago. That header beam is three degrees away from collapsing and crushing you flat."

"I inherited this place." I shoved my chin up, refusing to look away from his dark, harsh glare. I wouldn't let this massive stranger intimidate me out of my own bakery. "It belongs to me."

"Right now, it's a death trap." He dropped my hands. He hooked his scarred thumbs into the thick leather of his toolbelt. "Pack your bags. Get in your car. You're leaving."

"Excuse me?" The air rushed out of me. My chest heaved. "You can't walk in here and tell me to leave my own property."

"I'm the contractor the city called to condemn this structure tomorrow morning." He stood exactly over me, his broad shoulders casting a long, dark shadow. "I'm telling you to leave before you get killed."

"No."

The single word hung in the freezing air between us.

He stared at me. He didn't yell. He didn't argue. He simply stood there, an immovable mountain of muscle and denim, entirely unaccustomed to being challenged by anyone, let alone a woman half his size.

"I'm not leaving," I repeated. My voice shook, but I forced my spine straight. I wiped my bleeding hands on the thighs of my jeans. "I'm going to fix it. I'm going to open a pastry shop."

He tracked the movement of my hands. He looked deliberately around the room. He cataloged the shattered displays. The leaking ceiling. The frozen pipes. The damp rot creeping up the walls.

"You're going to fix it." A dark amusement lit his harsh face, entirely devoid of humor. "You weigh a hundred pounds soaking wet and you can't even pull a single rotted floorboard."

"I'll figure it out." My pulse thrashed wildly against my throat.

"You stay in this building tonight, you freeze to death." He crossed his massive arms over his expansive chest. "The boiler is dead in the basement."

"I brought heavy blankets."

He let out a harsh breath through his nose. He reached into his jacket, his massive hand gently checking on the sleeping kitten one more time. The absolute contrast between his harsh words and his protective actions made my head spin. He unclipped a heavy steel flashlight from his hip.

"Go sit in that chair." He pointed the heavy flashlight toward a sturdy wooden stool near the front register.

"Why?"

"Because if you walk under that archway again, I'll physically carry you out the front door and lock it behind you." The threat rolled out of him low and rough. He didn't raise his voice. He didn't have to. He would do it perfectly easily.

I swallowed hard. My throat clicked in the quiet room.

I moved to the stool. I sat down.

He turned his broad back to me. He began inspecting the sagging archway, shining the bright beam of his flashlight directly into the cracking plaster. Dust showered down over his dark hair and his broad shoulders. He completely ignored it. He moved with a quiet, efficient grace that entirely contradicted his massive bulk. Every single movement was precise. Calculating. He wasn't just looking at the damage; he was completely dismantling the problem in his head.

The silence stretched out. Just the sound of his heavy boots moving across the floorboards. The occasional scratch of his pen against a small notepad he pulled from his back pocket.

Violent tremors wracked my body. The adrenaline completely faded, leaving me painfully aware of the freezing draft. I rubbed my arms, wrapping my fingers tightly around my biceps. My bleeding palms throbbed with a dull, steady ache.

He stopped writing. He slid the notepad back into his tight denim pocket. Without a single word, he marched past me, out the open front door, and down the snow-covered steps.

I sat entirely alone in the freezing bakery. My stomach sank heavily. *He left.*

Of course he left. The massive contractor who just barked orders at me realized this place was a complete lost cause and walked away. I was alone again. Just like always. The weight of the failing building pressed down on my shoulders, heavier than before.

I stared at my bloody palms. Maybe he was exactly right. Maybe I was stupid to think I could salvage this ruin.

Boot steps thumped heavily on the front porch.

He ducked back through the doorway. He carried a huge wooden beam easily over one wide shoulder. His heavy steel toolbox swung from his other hand. He didn't look at the door. He didn't look at the snow.

He dropped the massive toolbox onto the floorboards with a deafening crash. He walked straight over to me.

He stood over my stool, dominating my space once again. His calloused, dirty hands rested solidly on his hips, right above his heavy toolbelt.

"Do not move from that spot." He scowled down at me. "I'm fixing the header before the roof comes down on your ridiculous head."

Chapter Two

Handing Over the Keys

The sagging load-bearing header above the archway was a widow-maker.

Grady popped the rusted metal latches on his steel toolbox. The hinges shrieked in the quiet room. He pulled out a laser measure, snapping the sharp red dot from the damp floor to the bowing plaster above. Nine feet, four inches. The rotted pine groaned, buckling under the relentless pressure of a foot of mountain snowpack sitting on the roof. One bad gust of wind, and the ceiling would come crashing down, crushing everything beneath it.

Crushing her.

Inside his unzipped canvas jacket, the stray kitten slept against his chest. A tiny, vibrating furnace. Grady ignored the freezing wind whipping through the shattered front window. He dragged the thick six-by-six oak post he had hauled in from his truck across the warped floorboards. Splinters bit into his calloused palms. He welcomed the sting. The sharp friction grounded him.

He set a cast-iron hydraulic bottle jack beneath a temporary brace. He gripped the steel handle, pumping it with relentless, driving strokes. The cold air burned his lungs. Sweat broke along his hairline, trickling down his neck to soak the collar of his flannel. Muscle fibers tore and burned in his broad shoulders as he forced the stubborn jack upward. The rotting house shrieked in protest. Plaster dust showered down, coating his dark hair and his back in a fine white grit.

He did not stop until the ceiling lifted a fraction of an inch. Just enough. He kicked the oak post into the gap, aligning it plumb. He drew his framing hammer from his leather belt. Three brutal, driving swings buried the steel nails deep into the wood, locking the temporary support securely into place.

The immediate threat of death vanished.

Grady dropped the hammer back into its leather loop. He wiped his dirty brow with the back of his wrist. He turned around.

Maisie sat exactly where he put her. Perched on the wobbly wooden stool, her knees pressed tight together. Her thin sweater offered zero protection against the bitter mountain draft. Violet shadows bruised the delicate skin beneath her wide eyes. Dried blood flaked around her torn cuticles. She gripped an old metal paint scraper in her pale hands, her knuckles stark white.

She looked ready to fight him for the right to freeze to death.

A harsh, possessive instinct coiled tight in Grady's gut. The urge to drag her off that stool, wrap her in his thick coat, and carry her out to his heated truck was a physical ache. She was too small. Too fragile to be fighting a collapsing building on her own. But he recognized the fierce, defensive tilt of her chin. She was used to fighting alone. If he barked another order at her, if he treated her like a problem to be solved, she would bolt into the snow.

He needed to prove she did not have to fight him. He needed to build the safety with his own two hands.

Grady walked past her without a single word. He crossed the room, his steel-toed boots crunching loudly over the shattered glass littering the floor. He stepped out onto the snow-packed porch. The mountain wind bit at his sweat-dampened neck. He reached into the cab of his truck, grabbing his battered steel thermos, a thick roll of visqueen plastic, and a stiff push broom.

When he stepped back inside, Maisie had moved.

She stood near the display cases, her small shoulders hunched against the cold. She raised the metal scraper, aiming it at a patch of hardened grime on the glass. Her hands shook violently. The metal blade skittered off the surface, accomplishing nothing.

He closed the distance between them in three long strides.

He stopped inches behind her. The top of her blonde head barely reached the middle of his broad chest. The scent of vanilla bean, old sugar, and cold sweat drifted up from her hair, sinking straight into his blood. He set the supplies on the counter.

"Sit down." His voice came out a rough rumble.

Maisie stiffened. "I need to clean this. The grand opening—"

"Is a month away." Grady reached around her. He did not ask for permission. He wrapped his large, scarred hand directly over hers.

Her skin was ice. A sharp jolt of raw heat spiked up his forearm at the contact. He swallowed a rough sound. He worked his rough thumb over her bruised knuckles, prying her stiff, freezing fingers open one by one. She gasped softly. He ignored the sound, pulling the metal scraper from her grip and tossing it onto the counter. It clattered against the glass.

He stepped closer, backing her flush against the display case. He trapped her between his solid body and the wood. He stared down at her hands. The deep cuts on her palms from the broken floorboard stopped bleeding, but they were raw and red.

"You are running on fumes." He kept his voice low. He did not break contact, his rough callouses sliding over her delicate wrists. "Sit."

Maisie's throat clicked as she swallowed. Her gaze flicked up to his face, tracking the harsh line of his jaw. She did not argue this time. She stepped around him and sank back onto the wooden stool.

Grady unscrewed the cap of his thermos. Steam poured into the frigid air, carrying the bitter, dark scent of black coffee. He filled the metal cup to the brim. He walked over and pressed the hot steel into her palms.

"Drink it."

She wrapped both hands around the cup, absorbing the heat. She brought it to her lips and took a slow sip. Color rushed back into her pale cheeks. A tiny, ragged sigh slipped past her lips.

The sound twisted low in Grady's groin. He forced his attention away from her mouth.

He grabbed the stiff push broom. He turned his back to her and went to work.

He swept the shattered glass with brutal efficiency. The stiff bristles scraped across the hardwood, gathering decades of dirt, dead pine needles, and broken window panes into a neat pile. He fell into the steady, methodical rhythm of labor. Sweep. Gather. Shovel. Dump. He cleared the debris blocking the front door. He scraped the frozen mud from the entryway. He reduced the chaotic disaster zone into a manageable workspace.

Every few seconds, the hairs on the back of his neck prickled. She was watching him.

He could feel her tracking the flex of his back muscles beneath his flannel. He wanted her to look. He wanted her to see exactly what he could do for her. He tossed the last pile of broken glass into a rusted trash bin near the door.

Next, he grabbed the roll of visqueen plastic and a specialized staple gun from his belt. He kicked a wooden crate toward the shattered front window and stepped onto it. He measured the gaping hole with a single glance. He unrolled the thick plastic, pulling it taut across the wooden frame.

Thwack. Thwack. Thwack.

He drove the industrial staples into the oak with rapid, punishing force. The howling wind outside slammed against the plastic, but the visqueen held firm. The relentless draft funneling into the bakery died instantly. The temperature in the room stopped dropping.

Grady stepped down from the crate. He brushed the sawdust from his thighs.

Maisie sat on the stool, the empty metal cup clutched against her chest. The frantic, terrified energy that had consumed her ten minutes ago was gone. Her shoulders dropped. The rigid line of her spine softened. Her breathing evened out, no longer hitching with panic.

She looked safe.

"Why are you doing this?" Her voice broke the quiet rhythm of the room. It was soft. Hesitant.

Grady walked toward her. He stopped a foot away, letting his towering height cast a protective shadow over her. He hooked his thumbs into his leather toolbelt, the steel hammer resting against his thigh. He looked down into her wide, exhausted eyes.

"The roof was going to crush you." He stated the fact plainly.

"That doesn't explain the coffee." She traced the rim of the metal cup. "Or the plastic over the window. The other guy I hired took a look at this place, demanded double the deposit, and never came back."

A muscle tightened in Grady's jaw. He would find the man who stole from her and break his jaw in three places. But right now, he needed to keep her grounded.

"I'm not the other guy." Grady reached out. He placed two rough, grease-stained fingers under her chin, tilting her face up. Her skin was so soft it made his chest ache. "You hire a boy, he complains about the work. You want this place fixed, you stand back and let me swing the hammer."

Her pulse fluttered wildly against his fingertips. Her lips parted. The scent of vanilla spiked in the air between them, sweet and sharp. Every instinct roared at him to lean down, to taste that sweetness, to back her into the counter and show her how much pressure he could exert.

Instead, he dropped his hand.

"The boiler in the basement is shot." He stepped back, severing the physical connection before he lost his grip on his restraint. "I'm going downstairs. I will get the heat running. Do not touch another piece of glass until I come back."

He did not wait for her to agree. He turned toward the narrow doorway leading to the basement stairs. The cracked concrete groaned under his boots. He descended into the dark, his pulse slamming a rough, steady rhythm against his ribs. He had a rusted boiler to tear apart. He had a shop to rebuild. And an exhausted pastry chef upstairs he was never going to walk away from.

Chapter Three

Calloused Hands and Caught Breath

The floorboards groan beneath my boots. The silence in the upper level of the bakery presses inward, heavy and oppressive. The only sound comes from the muffled, rhythmic clang of heavy steel striking iron from the basement. Grady went down into the dark over an hour ago. The ambient temperature in the room hovers just above freezing, leaving a dull throb in my joints. I huddle deeper into my thin sweater. I stare at the thick visqueen plastic stapled over the shattered front window. The material bulges inward, fighting the relentless force of the mountain wind.

My whole life, I have waited for the other shoe to drop. People rarely give without taking. They do not step into a chaotic disaster, brace a collapsing ceiling, sweep up shattered glass, and ask for nothing. The defensive, fiercely guarded part of my brain insists I need to chase him out. If I let go of the impossible weight I carry alone, what happens when he walks away? I will shatter faster than the broken glass currently sitting in the trash bin. I built my career in the city by fighting uphill battles without a safety net. I survived by refusing help, by never letting a man dictate my limits.

But listening to the steady, calculated strike of his hammer below, a dangerous warmth settles low in my chest. He fixed the structural beam. He stopped the draft. In a cardboard box near the register, wrapped in one of my spare shop towels, the stray kitten sleeps soundly. He stopped the chaos.

Financial ruin breathes down my neck. I possess exactly three hundred dollars in my checking account. My industrial ovens arrive in a week. I should be pacing the floorboards. I should be hyperventilating into a paper bag. Instead, the rhythmic sound of his tools acts as a bizarre sedative, grounding my frantic pulse.

The cold finally bites through the thin wool of my sleeves. I rub my arms, my torn cuticles stinging from the friction. I need to move. I edge toward the open doorway leading down to the basement. The wooden stairs are cracked, the edges worn smooth by decades of heavy boots. A single bare bulb swings from the low ceiling below, casting harsh yellow light across the damp stone foundation. Dust dances in the weak beam. The basement smells of old wet earth, rusted metal, and the sharp tang of ozone.

I stop on the fourth step down. The wooden tread bows under my weight.

Grady stands in front of the massive, rusted iron beast of the old boiler. He shed his heavy canvas jacket thirty minutes ago. Now, he works in just his faded flannel, the sleeves shoved high above his elbows. The shirt clings to his broad back, damp with sweat. A heavy leather toolbelt rides low on his hips, weighted down with hammers, wrenches, and thick steel pliers.

The brutal mass of the man defies logic. Thick, ropey muscle shifts beneath his sun-browned skin with every harsh turn of his wrench. His forearms are corded with heavy veins, dusted in dark hair and streaked with black grease. The heavy leather toolbelt rides low on his hips, drawing my gaze directly to the sharp V of his pelvis and the thick, powerful columns of his thighs encased in worn denim. He braces his wide stance against the concrete floor, immovable and raw. Every flex of his back radiates pure, unadulterated strength. A heavy heat pools low in my stomach. The man is a walking powerhouse of capability, tearing into the rusted metal with calloused, scarred hands that I have spent the last hour imagining wrapped around my waist.

He grunts, a low, rough rumble that vibrates straight up the wooden stairs and hums in the soles of my boots. Metal screeches against metal. He leans his weight into a massive pipe wrench, his severe jaw clenching tight. The tendons in his neck stand out like thick cords. He does not quit. He attacks the rusted problem with relentless, punishing force.

Clang.

Sparks shower the damp floor. The old iron boiler groans, a sound like a waking beast. A deep, mechanical shudder rips through the basement, rattling the rusted pipes bolted to the joists overhead. Water hisses somewhere deep inside the machine.

Grady drops the heavy wrench. It hits the concrete floor with a sharp crack. He reaches up. His thick fingers grip a heavy brass valve. He turns it with a rough twist of his wrist.

A heavy wave of ignition flares inside the cast-iron belly. The pilot light catches. The dull roar of burning gas fills the tight space, echoing off the stone walls.

Upward, through the floorboards, the rattling sound of the ductwork begins. Then, a rush of air pushes through the metal grates.

I reach my hand up toward the rusted vent hanging right above the stairwell. Heat. Actual, blistering heat blasts over my freezing fingers. The bitter chill clinging to my skin dissolves. The relief hits so hard my knees go momentarily weak. I grab the wooden handrail to steady myself.

"You fixed it." The words slip past my lips, breathless and quiet.

Grady turns. His broad chest heaves once. Grease stains his jaw, and a dark smudge of ancient rust marks his cheekbone. The bare bulb casts a severe shadow over his brow, putting the harsh, uncompromising lines of his face on full display. He pulls a shop rag from his back pocket and wipes his dirty palms, dragging the rough cloth over his scarred knuckles.

"The primary intake valve was seized solid." He tosses the rag onto a nearby wooden workbench. "Replaced the rusted threading. Repacked the seal. It will hold through the winter."

He speaks about saving my business like he just tied his boots. The impossible mountain of anxiety I carried since stepping foot in this town cracks down the middle. The upcoming grand opening. The missing ovens. The frozen plumbing. I spent weeks losing sleep over issues he just crushed with his bare hands.

I descend the final steps. The heat radiating from the boiler warms the room, but the heat rolling off his massive frame burns hotter. I close the distance between us, stepping over scattered tools, loose pipe fittings, and coils of copper wire.

He goes still. His dark stare tracks my movement, sharp and assessing. He stands a full head and shoulders above me, a looming giant in the cramped cellar.

"You should be upstairs near the registers." His voice is a low gravel rasp. "The heat rises first. You are shivering."

"I am fine." I stop directly in front of him. I have to crane my neck so far it aches just to look at his face. "I do not know how to thank you. The other contractor told me this boiler was beyond repair. He said it would cost ten thousand dollars to replace. Money I do not have."

"The other contractor was a lazy coward." Grady crosses his arms over his expansive chest. The movement pulls the flannel taut over his biceps. "You do not replace good iron just because you are afraid of a little elbow grease. It needed pressure and leverage."

My throat clicks as I swallow. "How much do I owe you for the valve?"

A dark scowl carves deep lines into his face. The muscle in his jaw feathers beneath the rough stubble. "I did not ask you for money, Maisie."

Hearing my name in his deep, rough voice sends a jolt straight down to my toes. My pulse kicks up a frantic rhythm. "I cannot just let you rebuild my shop for free. I have to pull my own weight."

"You pulled your weight the second you decided to stay in this town and fight for this building." He steps closer. The scent of cold mountain air, sharp sawdust, and masculine sweat rolls off him, wrapping around me tight. "My tools. My hands. You let me handle the heavy lifting. That is the deal."

I do not overthink it. I cannot. The heavy gratitude overrides every defensive instinct I possess. I close the final gap and throw my arms around his waist.

My face presses directly into the center of his chest. The thick fabric smells of dirt and hard labor. Underneath my cheek, his heartbeat thuds against his ribs—steady, slow, unbothered. It is the steady rhythm of a man who knows exactly who he is and exactly what he can handle.

Grady stiffens like he just took a live wire straight to the chest. For a split second, his thick arms hover in the air. The harsh lines of his body lock tight. Then, the hesitation vanishes.

His massive, grease-stained hands drop heavily to my hips. He does not just return the embrace. He grips my waist with his wide, calloused palms and lifts me straight up. My boots leave the concrete floor. The sudden shift in gravity forces a sharp gasp out of my throat. He adjusts his grip, pulling me flush against his rock-hard body until my face is level with his.

The physical contrast steals my breath. He holds my weight with zero visible effort, his thick thighs bracing us both. I grip his broad shoulders to steady myself. The muscles under his shirt feel like forged steel. The power dynamic slips from my control, but for the first time in my life, I do not panic. Safety settles deep in my bones.

"You fixed it." I dig my fingers into his shoulders.

"I told you I would."

He pins me with a stare. The space apart vanishes. The air between us goes heavy, thick with the scent of burning dust from the vents and the sharp tang of his heat. My heart thrashes wildly against my ribs. I want to surrender. I tilt my chin up, starving for the protection he offers.

Grady's gaze drops to my mouth.

He shifts one massive hand up my spine, settling his palm on the back of my neck. His calloused fingers tangle in my hair. The rough grip sends a hot jolt straight through my nervous system. He tilts my head back, exposing my throat to the dim basement light.

Then, he kisses me.

His mouth is hot and demanding. There is no hesitation, no gentle testing of the waters. He takes possession with the same raw, devastating capability he uses to tear apart rusted steel. I part my lips on a hitched breath, and he deepens the kiss instantly. The taste of dark roast coffee and masculine heat floods my senses.

I fist my hands into his flannel shirt. The friction of his rough stubble scrapes against my chin and cheeks. It grounds me. It is gritty and real and heavy with physical demand. His thumb strokes the sensitive skin behind my ear, a shocking contrast of rough callouses against delicate flesh.

A low groan vibrates deep in his chest. The sound travels straight into my body, igniting a heavy heat low in my pelvis. I wrap my legs around his thick thighs, anchoring myself to his solid mass. The movement presses my center directly against the heavy ridge of his arousal resting behind his denim fly.

He bites back a curse against my lips. His grip tightens on my waist. His massive fingers dig into the soft curve of my hips. He crushes me closer, swallowing my soft gasp as his tongue slides against mine. The slow, commanding pressure of his mouth demands my complete focus.

The kiss tastes like salvation. He is a man who builds foundations, and right now, he is building one beneath me. The frantic, exhausting need to survive on my own shatters. Giving this massive, capable man the control is not a weakness; it is the most intoxicating relief I have ever experienced. He takes the lead, exploring my mouth with deep, thorough strokes that leave my lungs burning for air.

He breaks the kiss to drag his mouth along my jaw. His hot breath sears my skin. He presses his face into my neck, inhaling sharply. The scent of vanilla bean and sugar clings to my skin, mixing heavily with his sawdust and sweat.

"Good girl," he rasps against my skin, his voice thick and rough. "Let me carry it."

I tighten my grip on his heavy shoulders. "Do not put me down."

"Not going to." He shifts my weight higher against his chest, keeping me locked flush against his solid body. He turns toward the concrete stairs. "I am carrying you up."

His boots hit the bottom step with a heavy thud. He carries me out of the dark.

Chapter Four

The Heavy Lifting

The mountain sun had barely crested the jagged peaks outside. Frigid light spilled through the thick visqueen plastic stapled over the front window, casting pale shadows across the warped floorboards.

Grady sat on a sturdy wooden crate behind the bakery counter. A battered aluminum clipboard rested on his thick thighs. He dragged a flat carpenter's pencil under a column of printed numbers. Maisie's business budget. She had left the open folder on the display case last night before collapsing onto the makeshift cot he built in the back office.

He studied the red ink. She was bleeding money. The former contractor had robbed her blind, taking a massive deposit and leaving a condemned ruin behind. Now, she was systematically slashing lines through her equipment wish list. *Double-deck convection ovens*—crossed out. *Commercial proofing cabinets*—scratched into oblivion. Beside them, in her tight, frantic handwriting, she had penciled in cheap, unreliable residential appliances.

A muscle feathered in Grady's jaw. He gripped the wooden pencil until the wood cracked softly under his calloused thumb.

She was compromising her dream to pay for a building that was actively trying to kill her. He was absolutely not going to allow it.

He set the clipboard on the glass counter. From his insulated thermos, he poured a steaming cup of dark, specialty roast coffee. He had driven his weighted plow truck forty minutes to the neighboring valley before dawn just to get the specific Ethiopian blend she had muttered about missing from Seattle. He wanted to give her the world. Right now, a hot cup of proper coffee and a structurally sound roof were the best he could manage.

Soft, rustling sounds drifted from the back office.

Grady turned. His pulse thudded a slow, steady rhythm against his ribs.

Maisie stepped into the doorway. She wore one of his spare flannel shirts over her clothes. The hem hung down to her kneecaps, swallowing her petite frame entirely. Her blonde hair fell in a messy, sleep-tousled halo around her pale face. Dark smudges still bruised the delicate skin beneath her eyes, but the frantic, panicked edge from yesterday had dulled.

She looked small. Fragile. But he knew the absolute titanium spine hiding under that oversized shirt. He was entirely obsessed with her. From the stubborn jut of her chin to her bleeding fingers prying at floorboards, she was everything he never knew he needed to worship.

"You are awake." He stood, his towering height casting a long shadow across the room. His work boots scuffed against the grit on the floor.

Maisie blinked, rubbing her eyes. She pulled the thick flannel tighter around her waist. "What time is it?"

"Just past six." He picked up the steaming mug and closed the distance between them in three long strides. He stopped a foot away, letting his broad shoulders block the draft funneling from the hallway. "Drink this."

She wrapped her pale hands around the warm ceramic. She brought the rim to her lips. Her eyes fluttered shut. A soft, indecent sound of pure pleasure slipped from her throat. "This is not the cheap tin coffee from yesterday."

"No." He kept his hands at his sides, curling his fingers into his palms. "It is the roast you were talking about last night. The one with the cardamom."

Her eyes snapped open. She stared up at him, her lips parted and glossy from the dark liquid. "You drove over the pass? The roads are completely iced."

"My truck has chains." He dismissed the effort completely. He would drive through a blizzard barefoot if it put that specific look of relief on her face. "Come here. We need to talk about the kitchen layout."

He guided her toward the display counter. Maisie's gaze landed on the open folder and the aluminum clipboard. The relaxed warmth instantly vanished from her posture. Her spine snapped straight. She set the mug down on the wood with a sharp crack.

"You went through my financials." Her chin tipped up. The defensive walls slammed right back into place.

"I looked at the equipment load." Grady leaned his hip against the sturdy counter. He crossed his thick arms over his chest. "You cannot run a commercial bakery on residential ovens, Maisie. They will burn out in three months."

"I do not have a choice." She dragged a hand through her messy blonde hair. "The structural repairs are going to eat the rest of my capital. The roof. The plumbing. The floorboards. I have exactly three hundred dollars perfectly clear right now. I have to cancel the commercial delivery."

"Do not touch that phone."

"Grady, be rational. I cannot pay for materials and labor and still afford the ovens."

"You are not paying for labor." He picked up the clipboard and turned it toward her. He tapped the broad tip of his carpenter's pencil against a new column of numbers he had drafted in the early hours of the morning. "I am doing the work."

She stared at the paper. Her breathing hitched. "I told you yesterday, I cannot accept free labor. I have to pull my own weight."

"And I told you your weight is building this business." He leaned closer. The scent of vanilla and sleep rolled off her skin, sinking deep into his blood. "Look at the sheet. The lumber for the floor joists? Salvaged from a cabin tear-down I did last month. The wood is perfectly sound, and sitting uselessly in my shop. The copper piping? I have extra coils from a commercial job in town. You buy the drywall and the paint. I handle the installation."

Her eyes scanned his rugged handwriting. Her throat clicked. "The header beam alone—"

"Is a day of my time." He dropped the clipboard. It clattered against the glass. He reached out, wrapping his large, calloused hands gently around her upper arms. The flannel shirt bunched beneath his grip. "I don't want your money, Maisie. I want you to keep the commercial ovens."

Maisie stared up at him. The fight drained right out of her. Her defensive posture crumbled, leaving her exposed and completely overwhelmed. "Why are you doing this? People do not just step into a disaster and fix it for nothing."

"I am not people." He slid his rough thumbs over the soft fabric on her arms. "I am the man who is going to make sure those doors open in four weeks."

She took a step closer. The gap between them narrowed to inches. She tilted her head up, her wide eyes locked onto his harsh features. "You are entirely unreasonable."

"I am practical."

"You are building me a bakery for the cost of a few cans of paint."

"You are going to feed me pastries until I burst. We will call it even."

A tiny, breathless laugh escaped her lips. The sound hit him square in the chest.

Maisie released her grip on the flannel. She reached up. Her small, delicate hand pressed flat against the center of his chest. Her palm rested directly over his heart. The steady, hammering rhythm beneath his ribs spiked.

"Thank you." Her voice dropped to a soft whisper.

Grady went perfectly still. He let go of her arms and brought his right hand up to her face. His thick, scarred fingers brushed a stray strand of blonde hair behind her ear. He let his thumb rest against the soft curve of her cheek. Her skin was incredibly warm. She leaned into his touch, a microscopic movement of pure surrender.

The urge to break the rules slammed into him with the force of a freight train. Every possessive, dominant instinct roared in his blood. He wanted to push past this cage of service he had built. He wanted to back her against the wall, cage her between his solid thighs, and kiss her until she forgot every problem she had ever carried. He wanted to claim her completely, right here on the dusty floorboards. The restraint required to keep his hands gentle felt like tearing a muscle fiber by fiber.

But she had been fighting alone for so long. If he unloaded the absolute magnitude of his obsession right now, she would panic. She needed a safe place to land, not another force trying to consume her.

He forced his thumb to stroke her cheekbone exactly once before dropping his hand.

"Finish your coffee." His voice rolled out in a rough, gravelly rasp. He turned his broad back to her, creating distance before his control snapped entirely. "The delivery truck for those ovens is coming in a week. We need to measure the kitchen layout."

He walked past the display cases and shoved through the swinging wooden door leading to the back kitchen. The space was a disaster of peeling linoleum and rusted prep tables.

He drew a twenty-five-foot steel tape measure from his leather toolbelt. He snapped the metal tab against the far wall and walked backward, pulling the yellow tape taut.

Maisie followed him. She carried the steaming mug in both hands. The oversized flannel swallowed her, but the determined gleam had returned to her eyes. The terror of financial ruin was gone, replaced by the fierce ambition that drew him to her in the first place.

"The double-deck ovens need a fifty-inch clearance." She pointed toward a corner currently occupied by a rotting wooden cabinet. "Plus a dedicated gas line."

"I ran the new gas line yesterday while you were cleaning the front glass." He locked the tape measure and noted the dimension on his notepad.

Her mouth dropped open. "You what?"

"I anticipated the layout." He released the tape. The metal zipped back into its housing with a sharp clack. He moved to the adjacent wall. "You need a prep station for rolling out dough. Preferably marble or stainless."

"Marble is too expensive." She took a sip of the coffee. "Stainless steel is fine."

"I know a guy in the next county who fabricates custom steel countertops for industrial kitchens. I will call him at lunch. He owes me a favor."

"Grady." She stepped into his path, forcing him to stop. She looked up at him, a completely bewildered expression on her face. "You do not have to call in favors for me."

"Yes, I do." He crouched down, extending the tape measure along the baseboards. The worn denim stretched tight across his muscular thighs. "Your job is to figure out the menu. My job is to make sure you have the tools to bake it. Stand back, you are stepping on the clearance line."

Maisie stepped back. She leaned against the doorframe, watching him work. She did not argue anymore. She just watched his hands, tracking the practiced, efficient movements as he mapped out her dream.

Grady marked the final dimension on the drywall. He slid the carpenter's pencil behind his ear. He had torn down the obstacle of her budget in less than ten minutes. The relief radiating from her was a potent, addictive drug. He would rip down every wall in this town if it meant she never had to look terrified again.

He stood, brushing the drywall dust from his thick fingers. He met her gaze across the empty kitchen.

"Grab your notebook, Maisie." Complete authority laced his rough tone. "Tell me exactly where you want the mixers."

Maisie hurried back to the front counter. She returned a moment later carrying her worn leather-bound notebook. She flipped through the pages, a crease forming between her brows.

"The primary mixers need to be anchored." She tapped her pen against her chin. "I have two eighty-quart planetary mixers coming. They weigh almost four hundred pounds each. The floor has to support the dead weight, plus the vibration when they run on high speed."

Grady walked precisely to the center of the room. He stomped his steel-toed boot against the linoleum. The floor gave a sickening, hollow groan.

"The joists under here are rotted through." He pulled his framing hammer from the leather loop at his hip. "I noticed it from the basement yesterday. If we bolt those machines down right now, they will tear straight through the floor and land on the boiler."

Maisie's face fell. "So we can't put them there?"

"I didn't say that." The familiar balance of the steel grounded him. "I said the joists are rotted. I am going to tear this subfloor out and sister new pressure-treated beams across the span. You will be able to park a cement truck on this floor by tomorrow afternoon."

"By tomorrow?" She stared at the vast expanse of the kitchen. "Grady, that is a massive job."

"It is exactly what I do." He pointed the claw of the hammer toward the rotting wooden cabinet anchored to the far wall. "That is where the stainless prep tables are going?"

"Yes."

"Then this garbage is in the way."

He strode across the kitchen. He did not bother hunting for hidden screws or delicate brackets. The cabinet was water-damaged and useless. He jammed the forged steel claw of his hammer beneath the baseboard, wedging it directly against the wall stud. He threw his broad shoulders backward, leveraging his entire body weight into the pull.

The wood screamed. Rusted nails shrieked as they tore free from the plaster.

Grady shifted his stance, planting his thick thighs wide for maximum stability. He grabbed the edge of the countertop with his bare hands. The corded muscles in his forearms popped against his skin. With one brutal, continuous heave, he ripped the entire ten-foot cabinet structure cleanly off the wall.

Dust exploded into the air. Wood splintered and crashed against the linoleum.

He stood in the wreckage, his chest heaving a slow, even rhythm. He kicked a broken piece of particle board out of the way. He turned to find Maisie staring at him, her mouth slightly parted, her posture completely frozen.

"What?" He wiped a smudge of dirt from his jaw.

"You just dismantled a kitchen with your bare hands." Her voice was breathless. A dark flush crept up her pale neck.

"I made room." He bent down, gathering the shattered pieces of the cabinet under one massive arm like they were kindling. "Keep mapping the outlets. You need 220-volt lines for the ovens. I will haul this out to the dumpster out back."

He carried the mountain of debris through the rear exit door, kicking it open with his boot. The freezing mountain air rushed in, carrying the scent of pine and impending snow. He tossed the wood into the rusted metal bin with a deafening crash.

When he returned, Maisie sat on an overturned plastic bucket, running her pen down a printed checklist. She looked up, chewing nervously on her bottom lip.

"The county health inspector." She tapped the paper. "He has to clear the building before I can legally turn on an oven. There is a whole section here on sanitary wall coverings and independent plumbing."

Grady walked over. He plucked the paper right out of her grip.

"Hey!"

"I know the health code." He scanned the list. His scarred thumb traced the printed lines. "Washable surfaces in the prep zone. I am putting up FRP paneling behind your mixers. Three-compartment sink. I already measured the plumbing drops for it. Dedicated handwash station. I salvaged a ceramic basin last week that will fit perfectly by the door."

He handed the paper back to her.

"You don't have to worry about the inspector." He held her gaze, demanding her absolute trust. "When he walks in here, he is going to find a fortress. He will sign the permit in ten minutes."

Maisie stared at the paper. Her shoulders slumped, an absolute physical release of a burden she had been carrying for months. "I have entire spreadsheets dedicated to stressing over this exact list."

"Delete them."

"Just like that?"

"Just like that." He hooked his thumbs into his toolbelt. "I told you. You handle the recipes. I handle the building."

"Have you eaten?" He stopped working.

Maisie blinked, caught off guard by the sudden shift. "I had coffee."

"Coffee is not breakfast." A dark scowl carved into his features.

He turned and marched out the back door again. He walked to his rugged truck parked in the alley. He unlocked the solid steel toolbox bolted to the bed and retrieved a thick, foil-wrapped protein bar and a bottle of water.

He returned to the kitchen and pressed the items into her hands.

"Eat." It was an order, low and uncompromising.

"I am not hungry—"

"You are running on adrenaline and caffeine. You weigh nothing, Maisie. If you pass out on this floor, I am going to wrap you in a blanket, lock you in my truck, and refuse to let you out until the grand opening."

She narrowed her eyes, a spark of pure defiance lighting up her exhausted features. "You wouldn't."

"Try me." He crossed his arms, his massive frame blocking the only exit. "Eat the bar."

She tore the foil wrapper open. She took a stubborn bite, chewing slowly while maintaining aggressive eye contact. Grady fought the dark amusement curving his mouth. She was vicious. A tiny, furious pastry chef ready to fight a man twice her size over a protein bar.

A fierce, possessive ache clamped around his ribs.

She swallowed. "It tastes like chalk."

"It has twenty grams of protein."

"I bake croissants for a living. I know what good food tastes like. This is an insult to my profession."

"Then survive the renovation, open the shop, and bake me something better." He stepped forward. He took the empty coffee mug from her free hand. "Until then, you eat what I give you."

Maisie took another spiteful bite of the bar. She sat on the overturned bucket, dwarfed by his oversized flannel, eating the terrible food simply because he told her to. The sight hit him with a profound wave of possessive satisfaction.

He was taking care of her. She was letting him.

"Finish that. Then grab a pry bar." He turned back toward the center of the kitchen, pulling his leather gloves from his back pocket. "You are going to help me pull up this linoleum before I sister the joists."

"I thought I wasn't allowed to do grueling lifting." She pointed the half-eaten bar at him.

"You aren't." He snapped the thick leather gloves onto his calloused hands. "But you need to hit something to burn off that stubborn energy, and linoleum peels off easy. You can supervise while I do the actual work."

"I am the boss." She lifted her chin. "I supervise by default."

"Whatever you say, boss." Grady pulled a pry bar from his belt and handed it to her handle-first. "Go to town."

They spent the next three hours side-by-side. Grady worked with ruthless efficiency, tearing up the rotted subfloor, exposing the dark, damp crawlspace beneath. Maisie worked the edges, peeling up the ancient, yellowed linoleum. She did not complain. She did not stop. Every time she encountered a stubborn staple, she gritted her teeth and fought it until the metal snapped.

His gaze tracked her from the corner of his eye. The fierce concentration. The slight flush of exertion on her pale cheeks.

He had spent his entire life building houses for people who never truly appreciated the foundation. They cared about the paint, the trim, the superficial finish. Maisie was down in the dirt, her hands covered in dust, fighting for the bones of the place.

He measured a length of pressure-treated lumber. He fired up his circular saw, the loud screech echoing off the bare walls. Sawdust sprayed into the air, coating his dark hair and his flannel shirt.

He shut the saw off. He dropped the cut board perfectly into place across the span. He grabbed his framing nailer and fired three rapid shots, sinking the steel fasteners deep into the wood.

He looked up. Maisie watched him. The pry bar rested against her knee. Her eyes tracked the movement of his broad shoulders, the flex of his back muscles under the damp flannel. The raw attraction in her gaze was absolute.

Grady held her stare, pouring the quiet, primal heat straight back at her. She needed to know exactly what kind of man stood in her kitchen. A man who built solutions. A man who did not back down.

"Hand me the next board." He stepped closer.

Maisie swallowed hard. She reached for the dense lumber stacked near her boots. Her fingers brushed the rough callouses of his hand as she passed the wood. Heat spiked straight up his forearm at the contact.

"Thank you." He took the board.

He turned back to the floor, driving the steel nails deep into the foundation.

Chapter Five

Anchoring the Frame

Dust hung thick in the bruised afternoon light filtering through the visqueen plastic stapled over the shattered storefront. Maisie wrestled with a warped sheet of half-inch plywood twice her volume. Flour coated the knees of her denim jeans, and a stubborn streak of white dusted her sharp cheekbone. She hauled the heavy wood backward, the rough edges biting into her torn palms, her boots slipping against the exposed floor joists.

Grady stood in the shadows of the hallway, a heavy framing square gripped in his right hand. A brutal, clawing ache tightened his chest. The urge to cross the room, pry the wood from her aching fingers, and bury her petite frame against his chest was a living, breathing obsession. He wanted to strip every ounce of her burden away and strap it to his own wide shoulders so she could just breathe.

He recognized her delicate balance. She wore her fierce ambition like armor, convinced she had to fight this collapsing building entirely alone. She expected every man in her life to hand her a bill or a bruised ego. If he pushed his absolute devotion onto her too fast, she would bolt into the freezing mountain air.

A sharp, splintering crack echoed through the room. The plywood slipped from her grip, slamming against the floorboards. Maisie gasped, her spine bowing as she sagged against the wooden door jamb. Her small shoulders hitched with a desperate, ragged intake of air.

The restraint snapped.

Grady dropped the metal square. It clanged sharply against the subfloor. He crossed the kitchen in three long strides, his heavy work boots shaking the dust from the rafters. He did not ask for permission. He stepped exactly behind her, his wide chest brushing the back of her oversized flannel shirt, and reached his thick arms around her sides. He grabbed the rough edge of the plywood.

"Let go." His voice rolled out in a rough rumble.

She stiffened, turning her head. "I can move it. I just lost my grip."

"Let go, Maisie."

Her fingers uncurled. He hauled the seventy-pound sheet of wood upward with a smooth, continuous heave, tossing it easily against the far drywall. It hit the studs with a deafening thud.

Maisie turned around. Her chest heaved. The violet shadows under her eyes looked darker in the fading light, and her bottom lip was chapped from the cold, dry air.

"You are running yourself into the ground." He hooked his thumbs into his thick leather toolbelt. "I told you to supervise."

"Supervising is boring." She rubbed her dirty palms against her thighs. "Besides, I need the prep area cleared. I have to test the hydration on the croissant dough. The ambient temperature in here is completely different from my old kitchen. If I do not adjust the yeast ratio, the lamination will fail."

She was exhausting herself over pastry chemistry while standing in a gutted construction zone. The absolute, unyielding drive in her possessed him. He wanted to build her a fortress just to watch her thrive inside it.

"The prep area is clear." He pointed a calloused finger toward the corner where he had set up a heavy plastic folding table earlier that morning. He had wiped the surface spotless and angled a portable halogen work light to bounce off the ceiling, providing bright, even illumination. "Test your dough. Stay out of the drop zone. I am laying the new floor."

They fell into a gritty, productive rhythm. Grady hauled stacks of pressure-treated lumber from the back alley, his muscles burning with a familiar, welcome heat. He laid the boards across the reinforced joists, measuring and cutting with ruthless precision. The loud screech of his circular saw drowned out the howling mountain wind.

The subfloor required absolute precision. He snapped a chalk line down the center of the kitchen, releasing a cloud of blue dust into the air. He measured the spacing for the new joists exactly sixteen inches on center. The old contractor had taken shortcuts, leaving the foundation compromised. Grady did not take shortcuts. He drove the three-and-a-half-inch framing nails through the dense wood, the repetitive, percussive strikes of his nail gun echoing like a steady heartbeat in the cavernous room. Every nail he drove was a promise. He was anchoring her dream to solid earth. He wiped the sweat from his brow with the back of his forearm, his muscles pulling taut beneath the damp flannel.

Every few minutes, his attention snapped back to the corner.

Maisie worked the dough. Her pale hands moved with practiced, hypnotic grace, folding and pressing the pale mixture against the white plastic table. She bit her lower lip in fierce concentration. The frantic, terrified energy that had consumed her yesterday was gone, replaced by a quiet, determined focus.

He tracked the exact moment her posture began to flag. Her rolling pin slowed. A subtle tremor shook her left wrist. She wiped the back of her hand across her brow, leaving a smudge of butter and flour on her skin.

Grady set his nail gun down on a scrap block. He wiped the grease from his hands using a shop rag, then walked out to his heavy truck parked in the freezing alley. He grabbed a fresh bottle of water and a thermal container of hot soup he had picked up from the diner two towns over. He had kept it tucked near the truck's heater vents to keep it boiling hot.

When he returned, she was staring blankly at a recipe notebook, her shoulders curled inward.

He set the water and the steaming container directly over her open page.

Maisie jumped. She looked up at him, blinking in confusion. "What is this?"

"Hydration and fuel." He unscrewed the cap of the water bottle and pressed the cold plastic directly into her palm. "Drink half of it right now. Then eat the chicken soup."

"I am not hungry."

"You are trembling." He reached out, wrapping his thick, warm fingers loosely around her delicate wrist. The pulse beneath her skin fluttered wildly against his thumb. Her flesh was icy. "Your core temperature is dropping because you have not eaten a solid meal in twenty-four hours. Drink."

She stared at his calloused hand, then up to the harsh lines of his face. She did not argue. She lifted the bottle and drank deeply, her throat working in the quiet room. A drop of water escaped her lips, trailing down her chin.

A dark heat flared deep in Grady's groin. He wanted to track that drop of water with his tongue. He wanted to back her against the folding table, drag his rough hands up her thighs, and consume her entirely. The urge was a physical pressure, heavy and driving. He forced his grip to loosen, letting go of her wrist before he bruised her with his need.

"Open the container." He stepped back, putting crucial distance between them. "I want to see the spoon moving before I go back to work."

She unscrewed the thermal lid. Steam billowed up, carrying the rich scent of chicken broth and roasted vegetables. Her stomach gave a loud, treacherous rumble. A faint blush crept up her pale neck.

"Thank you." She picked up the plastic spoon he provided. She scooped a small amount of the broth and brought it to her lips. She closed her eyes. The hot food hit her empty stomach, sending a flush of color back into her pale cheeks. Grady stood there, watching her take three more bites. He tracked the delicate movement of her throat as she swallowed. He needed to make sure she was actually fueling her body, not just humoring him.

Once she took the fourth bite, he nodded once.

"Eat." He turned his broad back on her. "I have to frame the back office."

He walked down the short, dark hallway to the rear of the building. The back office was a ten-by-ten square of neglected space. Peeling wallpaper hung in sad, curling strips. The single window was cracked, letting in a bitter mountain draft. It was miserable. It was entirely unacceptable for the woman currently working herself to the bone in the next room.

Grady went to work. He did not just patch the draft. He completely dismantled the problem.

He ripped the cracked window trim out with his pry bar, throwing the rotted wood into the hallway. He measured a fresh pane of double-paned tempered glass from his truck bed, sealing it into the frame with thick, weather-resistant caulking. The freezing air stopped immediately.

Next, he brought in his heavy portable space heater. He plugged it into the newly wired 20-amp circuit he had installed that morning. The thick orange coils glowed a bright, angry red, flooding the small room with intense, baking heat.

But the heat was not enough. He needed her to rest. He needed her off her feet. He refused to let her spend another night curled up on a wretched folding chair near the drafty front registers.

He walked out to his truck one last time. From the weatherproof toolbed, he hauled out a stack of smooth, sanded pine boards he had salvaged from a high-end custom cabin build. The client had discarded them for a minor color variation. To Grady, they were structurally perfect.

Back in the office, he fired up his portable drill. The sharp whine of the motor cut through the quiet afternoon. He did not just throw some boards together. He constructed a sanctuary. He measured the corner of the room, cutting the four-by-four pine posts to serve as sturdy legs. He assembled the frame using heavy steel corner brackets, ensuring the cot would remain entirely silent and stable under any load. He sanded down the rough cut edges with a block of coarse grit paper. He refused to let a single splinter threaten her soft skin. He ran his calloused palm over the smooth wood to verify the finish.

He unrolled the thick, insulated sleeping pad he kept for emergency winter shifts, spreading it over the wood. Over that, he layered two heavy wool blankets he had purchased specifically for her from the local mercantile before sunrise. The dark green wool was soft, smelling faintly of cedar and clean snow.

He stood back, wiping sweat from his brow. The room was no longer a damp, rotting office. It was a warm, secure vault. A safe place to land.

A loud metallic clatter sounded from the kitchen.

Grady dropped his drill. He was out of the office and down the hallway in two seconds flat.

Maisie stood by the folding table, staring blankly at a metal baking sheet that had slipped from her hands and crashed onto the floorboards. Scattered, raw croissants lay completely ruined in the sawdust and dirt.

Her hands hung uselessly at her sides. Her chin trembled. The absolute exhaustion she had been holding at bay finally crashed over her, breaking through her titanium spine. A single tear tracked through the flour dust on her cheek.

"I ruined them." Her voice was a broken, reedy whisper. "The lamination is wrong. The butter melted. I cannot even hold the pan."

Grady closed the distance. Her tears twisted like a blade between his ribs. He did not care about the pastry. He did not care about the mess.

"Step away from the table." He kept his voice low, gravelly, and entirely calm. He needed to be her anchor.

"I have to clean it up." She dropped to her knees on the subfloor, her small hands reaching for the ruined dough. "I have another batch in the cooler. I can start over. If I adjust the folding technique—"

Grady crouched down beside her. He caught her wrists, his calloused thumbs smoothing over her frantic, shaking pulse. He pulled her hands away from the dirt.

"Maisie. Look at me."

She squeezed her eyes shut. "I have to get it right, Grady. If I fail at this, I have absolutely nothing left."

"Look at me." He leaned closer, his tone carrying the uncompromising weight of a man who bent steel for a living.

She opened her eyes. The raw vulnerability in her gaze hit him squarely in the chest.

"You are not going to fail." He shifted his grip, sliding his large hands up her arms, feeling the delicate bones beneath the flannel. "But you are completely done for the day. You cannot build a business on a shattered foundation, and right now, you are crumbling."

"I just need coffee." She tried to pull away, a weak, useless gesture of defiance. "I just need to try again."

"No."

He stood up, towering over her kneeling form. The absolute width of his shoulders blocked the harsh glare of the work light overhead.

Before she could utter another word of protest, Grady reached down. He slid his left arm behind her back, his thick bicep pressing against her spine. He swept his right arm under her knees. With a smooth, powerful surge of his heavy thighs, he lifted her entirely off the floor.

The sudden loss of gravity forced a sharp gasp from her throat. She instinctively grabbed his wide shoulders, her fingers digging into the tough canvas of his jacket.

"Grady. Put me down."

"Not an option." He adjusted her weight against his chest. She weighed absolutely nothing to him. Carrying her felt entirely right, settling a deep, primal urge in his blood that had been screaming since the moment he met her. He turned away from the ruined pastries and the bright kitchen.

He carried her down the dark hallway. Her pulse thrashed a frantic, exhausted rhythm against his collarbone. She pushed against his chest, but her resistance was fading by the second. The heat radiating off his solid body enveloped her completely.

"I have to clean the floor," she mumbled. Her head dropped against his shoulder. The scent of vanilla bean and sugar drifted up from her hair.

"I will sweep it."

"The butter needs to chill."

"I will put it in the cooler." He stepped into the back office.

The heavy wave of warmth from the space heater washed over them. Maisie went perfectly still in his arms. She blinked, looking around the small room. The draft was gone. The harsh, peeling rot was hidden in the dim light. In the corner, the sturdy wooden cot he had built over the last hour sat waiting, piled high with heavy green wool.

"You built a bed." Her voice was breathless, entirely stripped of its defensive edge.

"I built a place for you to sleep."

He walked over to the cot. He did not drop her. He lowered his body, bending at his knees, and gently placed her onto the thick sleeping pad. The mattress yielded slightly beneath her weight. She sank into the soft wool, her eyes wide as she stared up at him.

He reached down and unlaced her heavy boots. His rough, scarred fingers worked the dirt-caked shoelaces with deliberate care. He pulled the boots off, dropping them heavily onto the floorboards.

He pulled the thick wool blanket up, draping it over her shivering legs, tucking it securely around her hips and up to her chin. The heavy weight of the fabric instantly settled the violent tremors wracking her petite frame.

Maisie stared up at him, her defenses completely dismantled by the relentless, suffocating care he was pouring over her. "You are running my entire life right now."

"I am handling the heavy lifting." Grady leaned down. His voice dropped to a low, rough rasp. "There is a difference."

He pressed his calloused hand flat against the mattress beside her pillow, caging her in. The scent of sawdust and his clean sweat hung heavy in the warm air between them. He lowered his face until his mouth was inches from hers.

"I am going to close the door. I am going back to the kitchen to scrub the flour off the floorboards. And you are going to close your eyes and let me take care of it."

"What if I need you?" The question slipped out, a raw, terrifying admission of her dependence.

A fierce, protective satisfaction flared in his chest, hot and bright. He brushed his rough thumb across her soft cheekbone, wiping away the last trace of flour.

"I will be right outside." He stood up, letting his towering presence fill the small room one last time. "Go to sleep."

Chapter Six

PREVENTATIVE MAINTENANCE

The solitary portable work light cast a harsh, yellow illumination over the temporary prep station. Midnight pressed against the frosted windows of the bakery. Grady knelt on the scarred floorboards near the front counter, a heavy steel tape measure locked in his right hand. He marked a length of pressure-treated lumber with his flat carpenter's pencil. The rough scrape of lead over wood cut through the quiet room.

The ambient noise of the mountain town had died hours ago. Snow piled high against the doorframe, sealing off the outside world. For the past three hours, a chaotic, relentless rhythm of clinking metal bowls and whirring blender attachments had echoed from the back hallway. Maisie was supposed to be resting. She had lasted barely forty minutes on the cot he built before raw stubbornness drove her right back to the folding tables.

Now, the mixers sat quiet.

Grady stood up. His knees popped in the freezing air. He shoved the pencil behind his ear and let the tape measure retract into its housing with a sharp metal snap. He wiped his dirty, calloused hands against the thick denim of his jeans.

Silence was a bad sign. When Maisie went quiet, she was either pushing her body past its breaking point or drowning in a fresh wave of panic over her budget.

His heavy steel-toed boots thudded against the floorboards as he walked down the narrow central hallway.

A disaster spread across the plastic folding table in the prep zone. White flour blanketed the surface like fresh powder. A metal mixing bowl lay tipped on its side, a sticky puddle of ruined dough dripping slowly onto his newly installed floorboards.

Maisie sat on an overturned plastic bucket.

Grady watched the exact moment Maisie's stubbornness finally lost the war against her exhaustion. Her delicate, flour-dusted cheek slipped off her palm, landing on the open pages of her recipe book with a soft thud.

A fierce, possessive ache seized his chest. She was so damn tiny—a fierce little blonde powerhouse trying to carry the blunt weight of a collapsing building on her narrow shoulders. His obsession with her wasn't just about the way she smelled like warm vanilla; it was a bone-deep, desperate need to systematically dismantle every single obstacle in her path.

He looked down at his own massive, scarred hands. They were rough, built for swinging hammers and tearing out rotted drywall, but their only real purpose now was to shield her. His greatest fear—the only thing that made his lungs tight with panic—was that she would work herself into the ground before she let him help. She fought his interference, terrified of owing him. But Grady didn't want payment. He just wanted *her*. Safe, rested, and thriving.

Seeing her shiver in the drafty kitchen, the urge to intervene overruled his hesitation. He wiped the sawdust from his palms and stepped forward, ready to carry her.

He stopped a breath away from her slumped form. The air around the table smelled of burnt sugar and exhausted yeast. He reached out. His thick fingers gently brushed the delicate curve of her shoulder.

"Maisie." His voice rolled out in a low, gravelly rumble.

She shifted. A soft, breathless sound slipped past her lips. She dragged her cheek off the thick recipe book, leaving a smear of white powder on the dark ink. Her eyelids fluttered, heavy and uncoordinated. She blinked up at him. Sleep deprivation had stripped her defensive armor bare.

She didn't jolt backward. She didn't square her shoulders to fight him off. Instead, she leaned into his towering shadow.

She reached out. Her small, pale hand pressed flat against his abdomen, right above the heavy leather of his toolbelt.

"You're still awake," she mumbled. Her voice was thick from sleep, her words slurring together.

"I am working." He kept his hands at his sides. His fists clenched to keep from grabbing her hips.

Her fingers drifted higher. She dragged her palm over the rigid muscles of his stomach, up to the broad expanse of his chest. The tough canvas of his work shirt bunched beneath her grip. She pushed her fingers higher, testing the dense flex of his bicep beneath the heavy flannel.

"You're built like a brick wall." She tilted her chin up. Her gaze dragged over his body, lingering on the thick, corded veins mapping his forearms. "It's distracting. The way your shirt pulls tight over your shoulders when you swing that hammer. I watch your back muscles flex when you rip down drywall."

A heavy heat slammed low in his pelvis. The muscle in his jaw feathered.

"Maisie. You are half-asleep."

"I'm awake enough to notice." She traced the jagged white scar running over his knuckles, her touch agonizingly slow. "It's so hot. Every time you crouch down to measure the baseboards, I can't look away from your thighs. You take up the whole room. I've never felt so small next to a man."

He stopped breathing. Her unguarded words poured pure gasoline over the possessive fire burning in his blood. She was staring at his scarred hands with naked, thirsty appreciation. She wanted his size. She craved his physical power.

"The other day, when you ripped those rotted cabinets off the wall..." She traced a soft circle over his breastbone. "I just wanted to touch your arms. I wanted to see if you were really that rock solid."

"I am solid." He stepped closer, caging her between his heavy body and the folding table. "And you are exhausted. We are going upstairs."

He didn't give her a chance to argue the point. He slid one massive arm behind her back, pressing his thick bicep against her spine. He swept his other arm beneath her knees, right behind the bend of her legs.

With a smooth, powerful surge of his heavy thighs, he lifted her straight off the plastic bucket.

The sudden loss of gravity forced a sharp gasp from her throat. Her hands instinctively flew up to grip his wide shoulders. She weighed nothing. Carrying her felt like holding a fragile bird, yet she fit flush against his broad chest. Her head dropped heavily onto his collarbone. The soft strands of her blonde hair tickled his rough jaw.

"My dough," she whispered, her eyes already sliding shut again. "The lamination is ruined. The butter melted out."

"I will handle the dough."

"I have to clean the floor."

"I will sweep the floorboards." He turned away from the bright prep station. "Your job for the night is done."

He carried her out of the kitchen. The dark, narrow stairwell leading to the second-floor apartment sat at the end of the hall. He had spent the morning reinforcing the dry-rotted treads, replacing the fatal hazards with fresh structural pine logs.

He took the stairs two at a time. His work boots struck the dense wood with a steady, commanding rhythm. Maisie burrowed deeper into his heat. She wrapped her arms around his thick neck, anchoring herself to his solid mass. The scent of vanilla bean sank directly into his lungs, grounding his frantic pulse.

The apartment above the bakery lacked basic refinement. Bare drywall surrounded a massive, open square of space. The original wooden floors were scuffed and stained black with age. In the far corner, a heavy cast-iron woodstove sat cold. Near the stove, he had dragged a premium twin mattress up the stairs two days ago, covering it in fresh white sheets and a thick winter duvet.

He walked across the room, his towering frame casting long shadows in the moonlight filtering through the uncurtained windows.

He lowered her onto the mattress. The springs groaned softly beneath his shifting weight. He pulled his arms out from under her, but she kept her small fists tangled in the front of his shirt.

"Don't go," she murmured.

"I am right here." He knelt on the floorboards beside the bed. He pried her fingers loose, pressing a rough kiss to her knuckles.

She was covered in flour and dirt. Grady refused to leave her in such a state. He pulled her battered canvas apron over her head, tossing the dusty garment aside. She wore a thin white undershirt and back leggings underneath.

He moved to the foot of the bed. He untied the stiff laces of her work boots, working the knots loose with his scarred thumbs. He pulled the heavy footwear off, dropping them onto the floor with a loud thud. Her wool socks were damp with cold sweat. He stripped the socks away.

He wrapped his massive, warm hands around her icy bare feet. He rubbed the thick pads of his thumbs over her soft arches, generating friction and heat. Maisie let out a soft sigh. Her tense muscles dissolved into the mattress.

"You fix everything," she whispered to the dark ceiling.

"I fix what is broken," he corrected gently.

He pulled the heavy duvet up, dragging the thick fabric over her legs, her narrow waist, right up to her chin. He tucked the sides tight beneath her petite frame, swaddling her in a secure vault of warmth.

He stood up and walked over to the cast-iron stove. He grabbed a handful of dry cedar kindling from the metal bucket. He arranged the rough wood with practiced, efficient movements. He struck a long wooden match against the stone hearth. The flame flared bright orange in the dark. He tossed it into the stove, watching the dry wood catch and burn.

Within minutes, a wave of heavy, radiant heat pushed the bitter chill out of the apartment.

He walked back over to the mattress. Maisie teetered on the edge of deep sleep. Her breathing slowed to a steady, rhythmic draw. Her pale face looked fragile against the crisp white pillowcase.

He crouched down one last time. He brushed a stray piece of blonde hair behind her ear. His rough, calloused fingers lingered against the soft skin of her temple.

"Sleep, Maisie." His voice was a raw, gravelly command.

She turned her cheek into his palm as she finally surrendered to sleep.

Grady held his hand against her face for another sixty seconds. He memorized the precise weight of her trust. When her breathing dropped into a heavy, unbroken rhythm, he carefully pulled his hand away.

He stood. He checked the iron latch on the woodstove, ensuring the fire was banked safely. He walked to the door, pulling it shut behind him with a quiet click.

He descended the dark wooden stairs. The ambient chill of the lower level hit him instantly.

He marched back into the glaring light of the kitchen prep area. The ruined dough still dripped over the edge of the plastic folding table. White flour coated the floorboards. The mess represented a glaring symbol of her stress, a desperate attempt to force success through pure suffering.

Grady reached for a heavy black trash bag.

He did not resent the mess. He craved the work. Every problem he eliminated was another layer of armor he built around her. He scraped the sticky dough off the plastic surface with a metal putty knife, throwing the ruined batch into the heavy bag. He grabbed a wet shop towel and scrubbed the table until the plastic gleamed flawless white under the halogen bulb.

He found a heavy push broom in the corner. He swept the flour into a neat pile, his broad shoulders swaying with the steady, repetitive motion. He scooped the debris into a metal dustpan, emptying it into the trash.

He tied the heavy plastic bag off with a tight knot. He hauled it out the back door, tossing it into the frozen metal dumpster in the alley. The cold mountain wind bit through his flannel, but he paid no attention to the freezing temperature. The possessive fire burning in his chest kept him driving forward.

He returned to the kitchen. He organized her scattered recipe books, wiping the residual powder from the leather covers. He carried the metal mixing bowls to the deep utility sink. He twisted the rusted faucet. Scalding hot water blasted from the tap.

His large hands dwarfed the fragile baking tools. He grabbed a thick sponge and scrubbed the dried yeast from the steel, stripping away the stubborn grime. She would not wake up and plunge her delicate fingers into scalding water. She would not scrub away her mistakes. He handled the grueling labor. He stacked the gleaming bowls neatly on the metal drying rack.

He moved to her prep station. He aligned her digital scale parallel to the steel edge of the counter. He found her worn notebook, the pages covered in frantic, scribbled notes about hydration percentages and failed yeast blooms. He closed the book. He left it resting on the clean table, placing her favorite black pen perfectly parallel to the binding.

By two in the morning, the kitchen was spotless. The threat of her failure vanished from the room.

When the sun crested the snow-capped mountains in a few hours, she would walk downstairs to a clean slate. She would not have to face her mistakes. She would only have to face him.

He shut the halogen work light off. Plunged in darkness, he checked the heavy deadbolts on the front doors. He stood in the shadows, listening to the quiet hum of the new boiler he had repaired yesterday. The building was secure. The foundation was solid.

He sat down in a sturdy wooden chair near the front entrance, crossing his heavy arms over his wide chest. He stretched his thick legs out, crossing his steel-toed boots at the ankles. He would sleep right here, guarding the door, waiting for her to wake up.

Chapter Seven

EXPOSED WIRES

The copper wire fought his grip. Grady bent the heavy gauge line with his bare thumbs, ignoring the sharp bite of the metal against his calloused skin. He screwed the terminal down tight with a heavy flathead screwdriver. The electrical panel sat in the dark shadows of the back hallway, but he worked by the harsh, singular glare of his portable halogen work light. He did not need perfect visibility. He knew the structural bones of a building the way he knew his own pulse.

A few feet away, the air smelled heavily of exhausted yeast, cold butter, and pure determination.

Maisie stood over the stainless steel prep station. Flour coated her apron in broad, frantic streaks. She dragged a heavy wooden rolling pin over a block of chilled pastry dough. Her knuckles turned white from the strain. She stood on her tiptoes just to get enough leverage to flatten the butter block hidden inside the folds of dough.

Every time Maisie sighed, rubbing the back of her flour-dusted neck, Grady's chest tightened like a rusted winch. He wanted to rip the weight of the world off her petite shoulders and carry it himself. Just crush her burdens in his scarred, calloused hands so she never had to worry again.

She was so fiercely stubborn, a tiny blonde force of nature trying to single-handedly revive this crumbling bakery. His obsession with her was not just about the sweet scent of vanilla clinging to her skin. It was a bone-deep, desperate need to be her sanctuary. He had spent the last three weeks rebuilding her joists, installing her custom ovens, and swinging his hammer until his muscles burned. He did it all just to earn one of her soft, exhausted smiles.

But the terrified independence in her eyes held him back. She did not know how to be taken care of. His greatest fear clawed at his throat. If he let her see the raw, consuming magnitude of how much he worshipped the ground she baked on, she would bolt. Or worse, once the final nail was driven, she would not need him anymore.

Across the kitchen, she swayed on her feet. She abandoned the rolling pin and reached for a fifty-pound sack of granulated sugar sitting on the bottom shelf of the storage rack.

Grady ignored the exposed wires dangling from the panel. Restraint snapped completely. He stepped forward. His heavy work boots thudded against the pressure-treated floorboards he had laid just for her.

He caught the thick paper sack before her fingers could find purchase. He hauled it upward with one arm, tossing the fifty pounds onto the steel table with a deafening metallic boom.

Maisie jumped. She spun around, a cloud of flour puffing into the freezing air between them. "I was getting that."

"You weigh barely twice what this bag does." He planted his wide stance in front of the table, effectively blocking her from the heavy lifting. "Tell me what you need on the counter. I will move it."

"I am perfectly capable of carrying my own sugar." She lifted her chin, refusing to step back.

"I know exactly what you are capable of." He leaned down. His broad shoulders eclipsed the glare of the overhead work light. "But you are not doing it while I am standing right here."

A low, structural groan echoed through the rafters above them. The wind battered the front windows. Dark clouds swallowed the jagged mountain peaks visible through the front glass. Snow began to dump fast and heavy, swirling in violent white sheets across the alley. The temperature inside the unfinished kitchen plummeted violently. A loud metallic clack sounded from the roof as the weather cap on the chimney rattled against the iron pipe.

Grady dropped his screwdriver into his leather pouch. He grabbed a roll of heavy waterproof tape and a thick sheet of plastic visqueen from his supply crate. He marched to the back door, securing the edges of the frame to block the bitter draft from killing her proofing yeast. He worked with brutal, calculated efficiency. He did not ask her to hold the tape. He did not ask her for a flashlight. He simply handled the problem.

He walked back to the center of the kitchen.

"The front pass is completely closed." He pointed a scarred finger toward the frosted glass. "We are losing the daylight, and the heating oil delivery has not arrived yet. The ambient temperature down here is dropping to single digits."

"I have to prep the patê à choux." She grabbed a wire whisk, her knuckles bone-white. "If I do not get the hydration right tonight, the eclairs will fail tomorrow."

"The eclairs can wait."

"No, they cannot waiting." She slammed the metal whisk onto the table. "You do not understand. If I fall behind schedule, the grand opening is ruined."

"The grand opening is secure." He closed the distance between them. He did not grab her, but he crowded her. His massive chest hovered inches from her drawn posture. "Look at me."

She stubbornly kept her gaze on the empty metal mixing bowl.

He lifted his right hand. He hooked his rough index finger under her chin, applying a fraction of pressure until she tilted her head up. He pinned her with a stare.

"I have reinforced every floorboard." His voice dropped to a gravelly rumble. "I have wired the commercial ovens. I have plumbed the sinks. You have the equipment, Maisie. The only thing currently breaking down in this kitchen is you."

Her throat swallowed hard. The fierce defiance in her eyes wavered, replaced by a hollow exhaustion. "I am just cold."

"We are going upstairs." He dropped his hand from her chin.

He marched over to the electrical panel. He flipped the main breaker, killing the power to the kitchen to protect the new equipment from storm surges. Plunged into gray shadows, the room felt instantly smaller.

He walked to the large pile of split cedar logs stacked near the back exit. He gathered a massive armful of the heavy wood, easily lifting a hundred pounds of timber against his chest.

"Walk." He gestured toward the wooden stairs with his chin.

She wiped her flour-dusted hands on her apron and marched past him. Her small boots hit the wooden treads with stubborn force. Grady followed right behind her, using his wide body to block the bitter draft leaking from the alley door.

The upstairs apartment offered a marginal improvement in temperature. The bare drywall and scuffed floors held a hollow echo. Wind howled against the single-pane glass, rattling the wooden frames.

Grady walked straight to the center of the room. He dropped the heavy load of cedar logs onto the stone hearth with a loud crash. He reached down and unbuckled his heavy leather toolbelt. The thick canvas and forged steel hit the floorboards with a heavy clang. He unbuttoned his insulated flannel jacket, tossing it over the back of a wooden chair.

Without the bulky outer layers, the raw, massive width of his frame dominated the tiny apartment. His dark gray thermal shirt clung tight to his chest and thick biceps. He took up entirely too much space. The physical contrast between his towering height and her petite frame instantly transformed the atmosphere in the room, trapping the heat and pulling the air tight.

Maisie stood near the small kitchen counter. She wrapped her arms around her waist. She watched his every movement.

He ignored the raw temptation of her stare. He grabbed the iron handle of the heavy woodstove in the corner. He threw open the door and loaded thick, split logs of cedar into the firebox. He struck a match against the stone hearth. The dry bark caught instantly. Flames licked up the chimney pipe, casting an erratic orange glow across the bare walls.

He closed the iron door and locked the latch.

Radiant heat pushed against the bitter cold.

Grady stood up. He turned to face her.

Maisie had not moved. Her blonde hair hung in messy waves around her pale face. The oversized sweater she wore swallowed her narrow shoulders.

"You are staring." He stepped closer.

"You took over my kitchen." She dropped her arms, lifting her chin. She took a deliberate step toward him. "You took over my renovations. Now you are taking over my schedule. You are entirely too demanding."

He did not move. He let her approach. He watched the subtle shift in her posture. The fear of his massive size was gone. She was testing the boundaries. She wanted to know what happened when she pushed back against a force of nature.

"I demand you stay alive." He crossed his thick arms over his chest. "It is a low bar, Maisie."

"I was not dying. I was measuring flour." She stopped exactly one foot away from him. She craned her neck to look up at his harsh features. "You treat me like I am made of glass."

"You are made of stubbornness and sleep deprivation."

"I am the business owner." She poked her delicate index finger directly into the center of his chest. The solid wall of muscle beneath his thermal shirt did not yield. "You cannot order me around."

A dark amusement lit his face. His mouth curved.

"Are you laughing at me?" Her eyes flared wide.

"I am admiring your complete lack of self-preservation." He dropped his arms. Before she could pull her hand back, he caught her wrist. His thick, scarred fingers wrapped loosely around her delicate bones. He pulled her forward.

She stumbled a half-step, landing flush against his solid torso. He spread his thick thighs, anchoring his stance. He brought his free hand to her waist, his wide palm splaying over the curve of her hip.

The sudden proximity erased the argument from her lips. Her chest caved as the air rushed out of her lungs.

"You do not own the bakery," she whispered, her voice fracturing.

"No." He slid his palm upward, his rough thumb tracking the soft line of her ribs through the thick sweater. He felt the rapid, fluttering beat of her pulse. "But I am the only reason the roof is still attached to the walls. And I am the man who is going to stand between you and this storm."

Maisie refused to look away. The heat from the woodstove rolled over them, but it was nothing compared to the searing heat radiating from his skin. She brought her free hand up, resting it cautiously against his collarbone.

"Why are you doing this, Grady?" The question hung in the quiet room, stripped entirely of her usual defiance. Raw vulnerability bled into her words. "You have spent weeks rebuilding this place. You refuse my money. You fix everything before I even ask. What do you actually want?"

His chest tightened. The terrifying truth sat right on the tip of his tongue. He wanted to drag her to the mattress across the room. He wanted to strip away the flour-dusted sweater and worship every inch of her soft, exhausted body until she forgot every problem she ever had. He wanted to build her a life with his bare hands.

"I want you to succeed." He kept his tone a low, rough rasp. He released her wrist, moving his hand to her lower back. He pressed her closer, eliminating the remaining space between them. Her soft thighs brushed the rough denim of his jeans. "I want you to stop fighting battles you do not have to fight."

"I have to fight." She gripped the fabric of his shirt. "Contractors always leave. The last one took my deposit and left the roof caved in. The bank is waiting for me to fail. You are building me a perfectly wired kitchen right now, but you are going to finish the job eventually. If everything is fixed, and the bakery opens, and the work is done... what happens then?"

The fear. It was not just his fear. She felt it too. She was terrified of the silence after the hammer stopped swinging.

"Do you think I am going to pack up my tools and leave?" he asked.

"I do not know."

He gripped her waist tightly. He lifted her straight off the floorboards.

Maisie gasped, her hands scrambling for purchase on his broad shoulders. He carried her two steps and set her down on the heavy wooden dining table occupying the center of the room. The thick oak groaned slightly under the sudden weight shift.

She sat on the edge of the wood, her feet dangling inches off the ground.

Grady stepped perfectly between her parted thighs. He brought his massive body flush against hers, caging her completely against the edge of the table. He wrapped his hands around the back of her thighs, his calloused thumbs digging into the soft denim of her jeans.

"I am not a contractor you hired." He leaned over her, his shadow swallowing her completely. "I am a permanent fixture. I am not leaving, Maisie."

"You will run out of broken things to fix." She swallowed hard. The scent of vanilla and burnt sugar rose from the crook of her neck.

"Then I will maintain the foundation."

He brushed the messy blonde hair away from her face. He cupped her jaw. The thick white scars mapping his knuckles scraped gently against her delicate skin. He tipped her face up until her mouth hovered an inch below his.

"I will build you custom display cases." He brushed his thumb over her bottom lip. She parted her lips, drawing in a ragged breath. "I will chop the firewood for this stove every winter. I will haul the fifty-pound sacks of sugar until my back gives out."

She closed her eyes. A soft, desperate sound slipped from her throat. "Grady."

"Look at me."

Her eyes fluttered open. The raw hunger in her gaze was an open invitation.

He lowered his mouth to her jawline. He pressed an open-mouthed kiss below her ear. He inhaled sharply, dragging the scent of her deep into his lungs. She tasted like sugar and pure determination.

"You take everything on yourself," he whispered against her skin. He dragged his lips down the column of her neck, feeling the frantic leap of her pulse against his mouth.

Maisie buried her small hands in his dark hair. She held on tight. "I have never had anyone carry the weight for me."

"Give it to me." He nipped at the soft skin where her neck met her shoulder. "Drop the weight right now."

She arched into his touch. Her spine curved. Her hands slid down to his wide back, her fingers tracing the heavy cords of muscle beneath his shirt. She pulled him closer, dragging his hips flush against the apex of her thighs.

The hard ridge of his arousal pressed aggressively against her. The thick denim offered zero protection from the blunt physical fact of his desire.

She gasped against his shoulder. Her hands froze on his back.

Grady went perfectly still. He pulled his mouth away from her neck, but he did not step back. He stayed locked between her thighs, forcing her to feel exactly what she did to him.

"You are massive," she whispered, her voice completely breathless.

"I am." He kept his hands firmly clamped on her thighs, holding her completely still against the edge of the table. "And I am completely at your mercy."

The blazing fire against the iron grate popped, a loud crack echoing in the silent room. The wind shrieked outside, hurling icy snow against the glass panes. Inside the small apartment, the temperature spiked to a fever pitch.

"I do not want you to be at my mercy," she breathed out, her fingers curling tight into the fabric of his shirt.

"Good." He lifted his right hand. He slid his fingers into the soft hair at the nape of her neck, tilting her head back. "Because I want to take care of you."

He brought his mouth down on hers.

The kiss was a total consumption. He did not ask for permission. He conquered. His rough lips slanted over hers, demanding access. Maisie opened for him instantly. He swept his tongue inside, tasting the dark coffee and sweet sugar on her breath.

She poured her absolute exhaustion and fierce ambition right back into him, meeting the aggressive stroke of his tongue with desperate heat. She wrapped her arms securely around his thick neck, holding him tightly.

Grady groaned, a low, primal sound vibrating deep in his chest. He tightened his grip on the back of her thighs, dragging her an inch closer until the friction forced a sharp, broken moan right out of her mouth.

"You take me so well," he rasped against her lips.

He broke the kiss just enough to let her lungs drag in air. He kept his forehead pressed flush against hers. The rough stubble on his jaw scraped the soft skin of her chin.

"I am stripping away every broken board," he promised strictly. He smoothed his wide hands over her waist, mapping the curve of her hips. "You are just going to bake, Maisie. You are going to bake, and you are going to let me worship the ground you stand on."

Maisie dragged her thumbs along his scarred cheekbones. The fierce independence in her eyes finally cracked wide open, leaving behind pure, unadulterated trust.

"Then start pulling the nails."

Chapter Eight

In Capable Hands

The blizzard outside sounds like a freight train derailing against the mountain. Wind shrieks through the towering pines, hurling sheets of dense white snow against the single-pane frosted glass of the upstairs apartment. Every wooden beam in the old bakery groans under the relentless winter assault.

I stand freezing in the tiny, outdated kitchenette. I clutch a rusted steel wrench in my trembling hands, staring hopelessly at the dripping copper pipe tucked under the ancient porcelain sink. Water steadily pools onto the scuffed floorboards, soaking through my thick wool socks.

The main pass is closed. The delivery trucks carrying my custom stand mixers are stuck on the other side of the ridge. My grand opening is sitting directly in the crosshairs of this storm, and now, the apartment plumbing is actively failing. I drop to my knees, shoving my arms under the dark cabinet. I clamp the wrench over the leaking valve. I pull with all my strength.

The rusted metal does not budge a single millimeter.

A frustrated sob crawls up my throat. I bite it back. I have to fix this. The bank will repossess the ruined building downstairs if I miss my opening targets. I adjust my grip and throw my entire body weight against the wrench.

A massive, calloused hand suddenly wraps over mine.

"Stop."

Grady crouches directly behind me. The staggering size of the man instantly shrinks the tiny kitchenette. He entirely blocks the harsh draft leaking from the frosted window.

Reaching around my waist, he securely grips the unyielding steel wrench. His thick, scarred fingers completely swallow my pale hands. The contrast is absolute—my skin dusted with residual baking flour, his knuckles marred by white scars and deeply ingrained sawdust. He easily twists the tool. The rusted valve shrieks, protesting for a fraction of a second before yielding to his brute physical power. The dripping water instantly stops. He gives it one final, decisive crank, securing the seal completely.

I drop my arms, staring at the dry pipe. "I was trying to turn it."

"You were stripping the threading." He tosses the wrench onto the counter with a loud clank. Sliding his thick arms under my armpits, he hauls me straight up from the wet floorboards. The sudden loss of gravity forces a sharp gasp right out of my throat. I instinctively grab his solid forearms to steady myself.

He turns me around. Backing me up, he forces my spine flush against the solid edge of the kitchen counter. He steps perfectly between my parted feet, trapping me against the cabinets.

The radiant heat coming off his dense body rivals the cast-iron stove burning in the corner of the room. I look up, craning my neck to meet his harsh facial features. He wears a dark gray thermal shirt that stretches punishingly tight across his chest, and a pair of worn, sawdust-stained denim jeans.

"I was handling it," I lie, my voice completely breathless.

"You were freezing your hands off." He reaches down, grabbing a dry towel from the drawer. Crouching low to the ground, he efficiently wipes up the puddle on the floorboards. Watching his wide back muscles flex beneath the thermal fabric sends a violent flutter of heat straight to my core. The man builds fortresses out of rotted wood. He reinforces shattered foundations. And right now, he is wiping up my kitchen floor so I do not have to stand in a puddle.

Standing back up, he drops the damp towel in the sink. He crowds me against the counter again.

"The road is closed, Maisie." Resting his massive hands on the counter on either side of my hips, he cages me completely. "I spent the entire night on the phone with the road crews. I have a buddy with a heavy-duty plow truck standing by the minute the wind dies down. We will get your mixers. The opening is secure."

I chew on my bottom lip. He eliminated my biggest logistical problem while I was attempting to sleep. "You cannot keep doing this."

"Doing what?"

"Rescuing me. Swooping in and handling the grueling labor." I press my palms flat against the unyielding muscle of his chest. "I am the business owner. I am supposed to be in charge. If everything is fixed, what happens next?"

A dark amusement lights his face. The corner of his mouth curves. "You are in charge of the pastry. I am in charge of you. And I am never going to run out of ways to take care of you."

The possessive weight of his words utterly destroys my remaining defenses.

Lifting his right hand from the counter, he hooks a rough index finger under my chin. He applies gentle pressure until I look up at him again.

"I want to take the edge off." He brushes his thumb across my lower lip. "Let me show you exactly what happens next."

I have spent my entire life bracing for the roof to cave in. Even now, standing in the dim light of the bakery's upstairs apartment, my instinct is to hold the walls up myself. But Grady is crowding me against the counter, his discarded leather toolbelt sitting near the door, and for the first time, my fear is not about failing. My fear is about letting go.

If I let him do this—if I surrender to the calloused hands currently gripping my hips—I am entirely at his mercy. I am so used to fighting, to surviving on exhausted willpower, that the idea of simply *receiving* pleasure feels terrifyingly vulnerable. He is massive, his broad shoulders easily bracketing my petite frame, yet he handles me with the same quiet, meticulous reverence he uses to rebuild my shattered life.

He looks up at me, his eyes dark and steady, asking for absolutely nothing in return. That is the most dangerous part. He does not want to conquer me; he wants to worship me. The fierce, desperate desire pooling in my belly finally eclipses the panic. I let out a shaky breath, my fingers tangling in his thick hair, and finally, completely, I let him take over.

"Okay," I whisper.

Wasting no time, he slides his rough hands under the hem of my oversized, flour-dusted sweater. The contrast of his battered skin against my soft stomach forces a sharp inhale out of me. Pushing the thick wool up, he waits for me to lift my arms in blind obedience. He pulls the garment over my head and drops it onto the floorboards.

I stand trembling in my thin cotton undershirt and denim jeans. The firelight paints warm orange shadows across his concentrated face.

Working with deliberate, uncompromising focus, he unbuttons my jeans. Gripping the brass zipper, he pulls it down with a sharp rasp. He hooks his thumbs into the waistband and drags the denim down my legs. He takes my wet wool socks with them, stripping me completely bare from the waist down.

Scooping me easily into his arms, he carries me the short distance to the premium mattress we dragged near the woodstove last night. He sets me down gently on the edge of the bed.

The cool air of the drafty apartment brushes my exposed thighs. It lasts only a second. Grady shifts forward, parting my knees with his solid forearms. He steps his wide knees flush against the edge of the mattress, sinking into the space between my legs.

The staggering size of his frame eclipses the rest of the room. He is a mountain of muscle and scarred knuckles, crouching before me like a devotee at an altar.

Resting his large hands on my bare thighs, his thumbs stroke the soft skin just above my knees. "You carry so much tension right here."

"I am a mess," I whisper, my voice catching. "I have flour in my hair. I have not showered since yesterday morning."

"You are perfect." Leaning down, he presses an open-mouthed kiss to the inside of my right knee. "And you are going to forget about the bakery for the next hour."

Trailing blistering kisses up the inside of my thigh, his dark scruff scratches slightly against my sensitive skin. The fiery friction makes my toes curl into the blankets. I fall back onto the pillows, my spine bowing off the mattress.

Reaching the apex of my thighs, his hot breath fans across my damp center. The raw anticipation makes my pulse drum a frantic rhythm against my collarbone.

"Open wider," he commands softly.

I obey. Spreading my legs further, I give him absolute access.

Grady lowers his head. His tongue darts out, tracing the swollen pink flesh with agonizing precision.

The first wet stroke pulls a broken moan from my lips. His mouth is entirely hot. Lapping at my entrance, he tastes the slick moisture pooling there. Then, parting my folds with his rough thumbs, he drags his tongue deep.

My lungs burn for air. I grip the white bedsheets, twisting the cotton fabric in my fists. "Grady."

"I am right here." Speaking the words directly against my wetness, the vibration sends a wicked shockwave straight through my body.

He settles into a ruthless, driving rhythm. His tongue flicks and swirls over the ultra-sensitive bundle of nerves with the exact same tireless stamina he uses to swing a framing hammer. Applying just the right amount of suction, he draws the swollen nub into his mouth and pulls strictly until my hips buck off the mattress.

"You take me so well," he groans. Pulling back just enough to look at my slick, glistening core, his gaze traces my flushed skin. "So sweet."

I cannot form a coherent sentence. My head thrashes against the pillow. Every swipe of his tongue unravels another knot of stress, melting the terror of failing right out of my bones. He knows exactly how to deconstruct my defenses. He systematically dismantles every barrier I have built over the past decade, replacing my deeply ingrained panic with pure, unadulterated comfort.

Lifting his right hand, two thick, calloused fingers slide over my drenched entrance. Without warning, he pushes them deep inside me.

The staggering size of his fingers fills me completely. The stretch forces my mouth open in a silent scream. Curling his hand upward, he strikes a deep, aching spot inside my body. He begins to pump his arm, sliding his thick fingers in and out in tandem with his devouring mouth.

The dual friction is absolutely overwhelming. The rough texture of his working man's callouses against my delicate internal walls creates an intoxicating, desperate heat.

"That is it," he praises, his voice a rough growl. "Give it all to me. Let go."

I am flying apart. Reaching down, I bury my fingers in his thick, dark hair. I hold onto him like he is the only tether keeping me on the earth. Drinking my wetness greedily, his tongue works faster, harder, faster.

"Please," I beg, my legs shaking violently.

"I have you." Pressing his thumb hard against my clitoris, he traps the nerve beneath his rough skin, and drives his fingers to the hilt.

The blinding climax hits me like a freight train. A ragged scream tears out of my throat, echoing his name into the hot, woodsmoke-scented air. My internal muscles clamp down violently around his thick fingers, milking his digits as wave after wave of absolute pleasure crashes over my over-worked body. I shatter completely around him, the white-hot sparks behind my eyelids matching the crackle of the fire.

Staying locked onto me, he drinks every drop of my trembling release. He swallows my broken sounds until my legs completely give out on the mattress. Slowly pulling his fingers free, he replaces the intrusion with a final, gentle kiss against my swollen center.

Standing up in one fluid, powerful surge, he easily scoops me entirely into his massive arms. He lifts my limp body completely off the edge of the mattress. My cheek lands against the solid wall of his chest. His heart thuds in a steady, calming rhythm beneath the dark thermal shirt.

Shifting us higher onto the bed, he pulls the thick winter duvet over both of us. He cages my exhausted body beneath his sprawling, unyielding frame. He brushes a damp strand of blonde hair from my forehead.

Looking down at my flushed face, his chest rises and falls with his heavy breathing. "You are mine to take care of now."

The fierce, terrified independence that kept me isolated for years finally crumbles into dust. I reach up, pressing my palm against the rough stubble of his jaw, and pull him down for a deep, lingering kiss. The man builds fortresses with his bare hands, but the safest place in the world is right here, entirely surrounded by his devotion.

Chapter Nine

Waking Without the Weight

She felt impossibly small tangled in my heavy flannel sheets, a streak of blonde hair spilling across my scarred bicep. Even in sleep, Maisie smelled like vanilla, powdered sugar, and the slick, hot aftermath of what we had done in the dark. My chest tightened. A fierce, suffocating wave of desire hit me so hard my calloused hands actually shook. I wanted to build a fortress around this bed. I wanted to frame the walls, reinforce the joists, and seal the doors so she never had to wake up and carry the weight of the world alone again.

But the pale dawn light creeping through the blinds was a threat. Fear, cold and sharp as a snapped floorboard, gnawed at my gut. Last night, she had finally let go. She had let me take control, let me worship her until she was trembling and breathless beneath me. But my fierce, ambitious baker was so damn used to surviving by herself. What if the morning sun brought back her armor? What if she woke up and decided last night meant she owed me something? I did not want payment. I did not want a transaction. I just wanted her. If she tried to pull away now, I did not know how I would survive it. I would tear down the whole damn mountain before I let her put those walls back up.

I slipped out from under the thick winter duvet. The drafty air bit my bare chest. I grabbed my worn denim jeans from the floorboards, dragging them quickly up my thighs and fastening the brass button. I left my boots in the corner. Barefoot, I walked to the kitchenette I had plumbed just yesterday.

Outside, the storm had finally broken. Blinding sunlight bounced off the massive snowdrifts barricading the frosted glass windows. The entire town was buried under four feet of dense, unblemished white. The main roads were completely impassable. She was not going anywhere. The realization settled the frantic pounding behind my ribs.

I pulled a cast-iron skillet from the lower cabinet. I set it on the gas stove, striking a match against the harsh stone counter to light the burner. Thick cut bacon hit the hot metal with a loud hiss. The rich, heavy scent of cured meat and woodsmoke filled the small apartment. I cracked three eggs into a glass bowl, whisking them with deliberate, even strokes.

On the counter, the coffee percolator bubbled fiercely. I poured a strong, dark roast into a heavy ceramic mug. I added exactly one splash of cream and a heavy spoonful of sugar, exactly the way she drank it when she was stressed over her recipe books. I plated the eggs and bacon.

I carried the hot plate and the steaming mug back to the mattress.

Maisie shifted against the pillows. Her eyelashes fluttered against her pale cheeks. She dragged her hands over her face, wiping the sleep away. She blinked up at me.

I stopped at the edge of the mattress. My grip on the ceramic mug tightened bone-white. I waited for the panic. I braced myself for the exact second she would realize I had seen her completely undone, completely vulnerable, and scramble to rebuild her defensive barriers.

The panic never came.

Instead, she stretched like a lazy cat. The thick duvet slipped down her torso, exposing the soft, pale curve of her shoulders and the tops of her breasts. She did not bother to cover herself. She looked right at me. A sleepy, challenging heat lit up her features.

"You are out of bed." Her voice was a raspy, morning-thick whisper.

"I am fixing breakfast." I knelt on the floorboards beside the mattress. I set the coffee mug on the nightstand and rested the warm plate on the edge of the bed.

"You are fully dressed." She propped herself up on one elbow. "Take the jeans off."

A violent jolt of heat hit my pelvis. She was not running. She was giving orders. The absolute shift in her posture completely derailed my brain. I stared at her, entirely paralyzed by the sudden authority in her tone.

"Eat first." I picked up the heavy steel fork. I speared a thick piece of crispy bacon. "You ran yourself into the ground yesterday. You need fuel."

She leaned forward. She did not take the fork from my hand. She parted her lips, waiting.

I fed her the bacon. My rough thumb brushed her lower lip as she pulled the meat from the tines. She chewed slowly, refusing to look away. I scooped up a bite of the scrambled eggs, bringing it to her mouth. She ate it right off the heavy steel. The intense, domestic intimacy of feeding her stripped away every lingering trace of my fear. She was accepting my care without a single ounce of resistance.

She swallowed the food. "The bacon is perfect."

"I can cook." I set the fork down on the porcelain plate.

"You can do a lot of things." She reached out. Her small, incredibly soft fingers traced the heavy cord of muscle running down my bare forearm. She dragged her nail lightly over the jagged white scar near my elbow. "But I think you are wearing too many clothes right now."

"Maisie." My voice dropped an entire octave, morphing into a rough growl.

She pushed the heavy duvet all the way down to her waist. Her breasts were completely bare, the pale pink peaks tightly pebbled in the cool air of the apartment. "You said you were going to handle the heavy lifting today. I am waiting."

I shoved the plate onto the nightstand. The ceramic clattered loudly against the wood.

I gripped the brass button of my jeans, ripping it open. I dragged the denim down my thighs, kicking the heavy fabric onto the floorboards. I was completely hard, an aching, desperate pressure pooling in my groin.

I climbed onto the mattress. The springs groaned under my massive weight.

Maisie fell back onto the pillows. She spread her legs, offering absolute, unrestricted access. The sweet, musky scent of her arousal hit my senses, totally overriding my control. I crawled between her parted thighs. I braced my wide shoulders over her hips, caging her entirely beneath my heavy frame.

"I am going to take care of you," I promised strictly.

I dragged my hands up her soft calves, my rough callouses catching slightly on her smooth skin. I pushed her knees wider, opening her completely to the cold morning air. Her core was perfectly flushed, slick and glistening with wetness.

I lowered my head.

I pressed an open-mouthed kiss to the soft skin of her inner thigh. She hitched a sharp breath. I dragged my mouth higher. I buried my face directly into her wetness.

My tongue darted out, dragging in a long, deliberate stripe straight up her slit.

Maisie arched violently off the mattress. Her fingers instantly tangled in my thick hair.

"Grady." Her voice fractured into a desperate gasp.

"I have you." I spoke the words directly against her swollen clitoris. The vibration of my deep voice made her hips buck.

I settled into the work. I approached her body the same way I framed a house—with relentless, uncompromising stamina and total attention to detail. I lapped at her slick folds, drinking her intoxicating taste. She tasted like heavy cream and pure, unadulterated need. I parted her petals with my scarred thumbs, exposing the ultra-sensitive bundle of nerves.

I wrapped my lips around her clitoris. I applied a firm, steady suction, pulling the swollen flesh directly into my mouth. I flicked my tongue against it in a rapid, driving rhythm.

Her nails dug half-moons into my scalp. She thrashed against the white sheets. "Please. It is too much."

"Give it to me." I tightened my grip on her thighs, anchoring her completely flush against my mouth. I refused to let her pull away. I wanted to consume every single drop of her panic. I dragged two thick fingers over her drenched entrance and pushed them straight inside her tight heat.

The physical stretch forced a loud, ragged moan right out of her throat. I hooked my fingers upward, striking the aching bundle of nerves deep inside her. I pumped my hand in tandem with the aggressive, devouring suction of my mouth.

The friction was absolute. She was so tight, milking my calloused fingers with every frantic thrust. I fed off her pleasure. It was a physical necessity for me to tear down her control and build her back up.

"You taste so sweet," I rasped against her wetness. I pushed my fingers deeper, stretching her completely open. "Let go, Maisie. Let me handle it."

"Grady! I cannot—"

"You can." I sucked harder, bearing down on the tightest point of her pressure.

She shattered. A blinding orgasm ripped through her petite frame. She screamed my name, a broken, euphoric sound that echoed off the bare drywall. Her internal muscles clamped down violently around my fingers, pulsing with relentless, rhythmic heat. Hot, sweet liquid flooded my tongue. I swallowed every drop. I stayed completely anchored between her thighs, licking her clean until the violent tremors wracking her body finally faded into soft, exhausted twitches.

I slowly pulled my fingers free. I dragged myself up the length of her body.

Maisie lay completely limp against the pillows. Her chest heaved. I bracketed her shoulders with my thick arms, hovering over her flushed, gorgeous face.

She reached up, her hands trembling as she grabbed my jaw. She pulled me down for a deep, lingering kiss. The taste of her own climax transferred between our mouths.

"You are entirely too capable," she breathed against my lips.

"I maintain the foundation." I kissed the tip of her nose. I pulled the heavy duvet back up, tucking it securely beneath her chin. "Stay in bed. Drink your coffee. I have a path to clear."

I walked out to the small upstairs porch an hour later. The bitter freezing air bit into my skin. The snow was piled four feet high against the wooden railing. The stairs leading down to the alley were completely buried. Delivery trucks would never make it to the back door of the bakery unless I dug out the entire loading zone.

I grabbed the heavy metal snow shovel I kept leaning against the siding. I wore my insulated work boots and a pair of worn denim jeans. I started with my heavy flannel jacket on, but ten minutes of grueling physical labor under the blinding morning sun had me sweating heavily.

I stripped the jacket off, tossing it onto a dry patch of wood. My dark gray thermal shirt followed five minutes later.

The freezing wind felt completely right against my bare chest. I jammed the steel edge of the shovel deep into the densely packed snow. I bent my knees, anchoring my wide stance. With a powerful surge of my thighs, I hoisted forty pounds of heavy, wet snow into the air, throwing it entirely over the wooden railing.

I settled into a brutal, steady rhythm. Scoop. Lift. Throw.

The repetitive motion engaged every muscle in my massive frame. My breathing turned heavy, pluming in white clouds in the frigid air. I cleared the top landing and began hacking away at the buried wooden stairs.

A sharp scrape of wood sounded behind me. The heavy apartment door swung open.

Maisie stood on the threshold. She wore my discarded flannel jacket over her jeans, the oversized garment swallowing her petite frame entirely. She held the steaming ceramic coffee mug in her small hands.

I stopped shoveling. "You should be inside."

She took a sip of the dark coffee. Her gaze dragged deliberately over my bare chest. "Do not stop on my account."

I rested my forearms on the handle of the shovel. I pinned her with a stare.

"I am serious, Grady." She stepped onto the porch. Her gaze was pure, unadulterated thirst, tracking the heavy beads of sweat rolling down my bare collarbone. "I am standing here completely mesmerized by the absolute width of your shoulders. The way your back muscles flex when you heave that heavy snow over the railing is distinctly distracting. You have these massive, thick thighs planted like tree trunks. And your hands..." She swallowed hard, staring at my scarred knuckles gripping the metal handle. "Your rough, calloused hands swinging that heavy steel shovel make me want to drag you right back to that mattress. You are built like a brick wall, Grady. Watching you perform grueling physical labor is doing thoroughly wicked things to my pulse."

A dark amusement lit my face. I wiped the sweat from my brow with the back of my forearm. "You want me back in bed."

"I have a business to run." She lifted her chin, though the hungry flush on her cheeks betrayed her completely. "But the delivery trucks cannot access that loading dock properly until it is pristine."

I laughed, a low, rough rumble in my chest.

"Spotless," she demanded playfully.

I turned back to the snowdrift. I jammed the shovel into the ice with renewed, aggressive force. I cleared the remaining stairs in record time. I systematically scraped the wooden treads clean, ensuring not a single patch of black ice remained. I refused to let her slip and fall.

I moved down to the alley floor. I carved a wide, structural trench through the four-foot snowbanks, building a secure channel leading directly to the back doors of the commercial kitchen. I squared off the edges of the snow walls. I packed the ice tight with the flat blade of the shovel so it would not cave in on her.

Forty-five minutes later, the alley was completely operational. The path was wide enough to haul a commercial mixer right up to the threshold.

I rested the steel shovel against the brick exterior of the building. I walked back up the wooden stairs. My boots thudded heavily against the cleared planks.

Maisie still stood on the porch. The cold wind whipped strands of blonde hair across her face.

I stopped on the top step. I stood exactly one foot below her, putting us perfectly at eye level.

"The loading zone is secure." I reached out, resting my cold, rough hands on her waist. The thick flannel of my jacket bunched beneath my grip. "The road crew will punch through the pass by noon. Your equipment will arrive."

"You fixed it." She stepped closer. She rested her hands on my bare, sweating chest. The shocking contrast of her warm, soft palms against my freezing skin sent a heavy jolt straight to my core.

"I fixed the snow." I pulled her against me. "You are the one who has to bake the pastries. The grand opening is tomorrow."

She did not flinch at the reminder. The crushing, terrified anxiety that had defined her entire existence for the past month was completely gone. She looked toward the towering, snow-capped mountains in the distance.

"I can handle the baking." She tilted her head, pressing a soft kiss to my jawline. "As long as you stay right here and handle the heavy lifting."

"I am not going anywhere, Maisie." I wrapped my massive arms completely around her, trapping her fiercely against my chest. "I am building my life exactly where you stand."

The winter sun glared bright off the freshly cleared pathway.

Chapter Ten

TAKING UP THE SLACK

My shoulders ached, a familiar throbbing from years of carrying every burden alone. If a pipe broke or a dream crumbled, I was the one who had to glue it back together with relentless, white-knuckled stubbornness.

Until Grady.

I stood behind the flour-dusted display counter. Grady occupied the center of the bakery floor. His massive, flannel-clad shoulders shifted as he effortlessly hoisted a custom oak support beam into place. The rhythmic, deafening *thwack* of his framing hammer echoed off the drywall. That heavy, aggressive sound should have triggered my fierce independence. It should have warned me about relying on a man who could easily pack up his heavy toolbelt and walk out the door.

Instead, it sounded like an absolute sanctuary.

Panic, sharp and biting as the mountain snow barricading the front windows, fluttered high in my chest. *Stop him,* my survival instincts screamed. *If you let this man bear the weight of the bakery, if you let him handle the grueling mental load, you will forget exactly how to stand on your own.* The terror of leaning on a massive, capable contractor was paralyzing. I did not know how to exist without the constant, grinding struggle.

But the agonizing, bone-deep physical urge to drop the heavy armor deafened the fear. Grady did not keep a ledger. He did not want a transaction. He just wanted to build a fortress for me to breathe inside. I wanted to surrender. I wanted to sink into his quiet, calloused strength and never claw my way back out.

He drove the final ten-penny nail into the oak beam. He lowered his heavy steel framing hammer, hooking it smoothly onto the thick leather loop of his toolbelt. He turned. The dark grey thermal shirt beneath his unbuttoned flannel stretched punishingly tight across his wide chest.

He wiped a streak of sawdust from his forehead with the back of his massive forearm. He caught me staring.

A slow, dark amusement lit his harsh features. "You are not measuring dough."

"I am supervising the structural integrity of my building." I crossed my arms, leaning my hips against the stainless steel prep table.

"The building is solid." He closed the distance between us in three long, heavy strides. His steel-toed boots thudded against the pressure-treated floorboards. He stopped exactly one foot away, his towering frame completely eclipsing the afternoon sunlight filtering through the frosted glass. "You are just avoiding the heavy bags of sugar in the pantry."

"I can carry fifty pounds of sugar."

"I know." He reached out. His incredibly rough, scarred fingers brushed a stray dusting of white flour from my collarbone. The light friction of his callouses against my skin sent a heavy jolt of heat straight to my core. "But I am standing right here. You never have to carry it again."

Before I could formulate a stubborn reply, a violent, metallic crack echoed from the back prep room.

The sound ripped through the quiet bakery. A violent hiss followed instantly.

I spun around. My boots slipped on the floorboards as I desperately scrambled toward the commercial dishwashing station.

The ancient, oxidized copper pipe feeding the main utility sink had completely ruptured. A high-pressure geyser of freezing municipal water blasted across the room. It slammed against the freshly painted drywall, ricocheting in a devastating arc straight toward the heavy wooden pallets holding my premium bread flour.

My throat closed tight. The grand opening was exactly twenty-four hours away. The road crews had finally cleared the pass. The mixers were operational. Everything was perfectly aligned, and now the entire ground floor was flooding.

"No!" I lunged forward.

I grabbed a stack of thin cotton bar towels from the prep station. I threw myself at the ruptured pipe. The freezing water hit me directly in the chest, soaking through my thin sweater in a fraction of a second. The bitter cold bit into my skin.

I wrapped the pathetic cotton towels around the jagged copper opening. I squeezed with every ounce of strength in my hands. The heavy water pressure completely ignored my effort. The freezing liquid blasted right through the thin fabric, spraying directly into my face and blinding me.

My hands shook violently. The water level pooled around my boots, creeping closer to the fifty-pound sacks of dry goods. A frantic, suffocating terror ripped out the oxygen in my lungs. I was going to lose the flour. I was going to fail the health inspection. The bank was going to repossess the building.

A massive shadow swallowed the glaring overhead light.

Grady did not yell. He did not ask what happened. He simply stepped straight into the freezing flood.

"Let go, Maisie." His gravelly voice held zero panic. It was a raw, immovable command.

"The flour—" I choked on a mouthful of cold water, my fingers cramping painfully around the rusted pipe. "The water is hitting the flour!"

He did not argue. He reached down and clamped his massive, calloused hands directly over my freezing, shaking fists. He easily pried my fingers loose from the copper.

He shoved me gently but firmly behind his wide back.

He dropped to his knees in the freezing water. His worn denim jeans soaked through instantly, but he completely ignored the brutal temperature. He did not waste time trying to cap a pressurized line with a towel. He traced the copper pipe straight down to the baseboard with his bare hands.

He found the ancient, corroded main shut-off valve hidden behind the base of the sink.

The rusted iron wheel was completely fused shut by decades of mineral buildup. Grady wrapped his thick, scarred right hand around the metal. The heavy cords of muscle in his thick forearm bunched tight. He ripped the wheel clockwise with brute, terrifying physical power. The rusted metal shrieked loudly, protesting the violent torque.

He gave it one final, devastating twist.

The high-pressure geyser instantly died. The aggressive hissing stopped. The only sound left in the kitchen was the dripping of residual water falling onto the flooded floorboards.

I stood frozen against the stainless steel counter. My teeth chattered violently. My sweater clung to my freezing skin, and my hands throbbed from the cold.

Grady stood up. Water dripped from his dark hair and his thick flannel jacket. He did not look at the ruined pipe. He looked entirely at me.

His jaw clenched tight. A dangerous, possessive fire burned in his dark eyes as he took in my trembling, soaking wet frame.

He marched past the puddle. He grabbed a thick, dry, heavy-duty moving blanket from his equipment crate. He closed the distance between us and draped the heavy material completely over my narrow shoulders.

He pulled the edges tight beneath my chin, swaddling me securely.

"You belong behind me," he ordered roughly. He reached up, his large, warm palms cupping my freezing cheeks. His thumbs brushed the dripping water from my cheekbones. "When a pipe bursts, when a framing board snaps, when the roof caves in. You step back. I take the hit."

"It was going to ruin the flour." My voice fractured, a pathetic, broken whisper.

"I can buy more flour." He pressed his forehead flush against mine. The radiant heat coming off his massive body cut straight through the bitter cold of my wet clothes. "I cannot replace you."

He dropped his hands from my face.

He turned back to the disaster zone. He walked to the center of the kitchen and grabbed his heavy steel toolbox. The metal clasps snapped open with a sharp clank. He pulled out a heavy pipe cutter, a wire brush, and an acetylene torch.

He knelt back down into the puddle.

I pulled the thick blanket tighter around my shivering body. I watched him work.

He did not complain about the freezing water soaking his boots. He did not sigh heavily or rub the back of his neck in frustration. He simply activated the torch. The blue flame hissed to life.

He clamped the metal cutter around the jagged copper pipe. He spun the tool with practiced, relentless efficiency, slicing the ruined metal clean off. He prepped the new fitting, his thick, scarred fingers moving with absolute, unwavering precision. He applied the flux, fitted the heavy brass coupling, and hit it with the blue flame.

The solder melted perfectly into the joint, creating an impenetrable seal.

Ten minutes. It took him exactly ten minutes to permanently eliminate the threat that had nearly sent me into a total panic attack.

He shut off the torch. He reached down and twisted the main water valve back open.

The pipes groaned as the pressure returned. The new brass fitting held completely dry. Not a single drop of water leaked from the joint.

Grady stood up. He tossed the heavy tools back into the steel box. He grabbed a massive stack of clean, dry shop towels from his supply bin.

He threw them onto the flooded floorboards. He dropped to his hands and knees and began wiping up the mess. The broad expanse of his back shifted under the wet flannel as he systematically dried the pressure-treated wood.

The crushing weight on my chest evaporated.

The terror of standing entirely alone in a flooded kitchen vanished, replaced by a deep, overwhelming wave of absolute security. The man did not buy solutions. He built them. He dismantled the chaos with his bare hands and shielded me from the fallout.

I dropped the heavy blanket onto the dry section of the counter. I walked across the kitchen.

I knelt on the floorboards directly beside him.

Grady stopped wiping the wood. He sat back on his heavy heels, his wide thighs planting firmly on the ground. "You are going to get wet again."

"I do not care."

I reached out. I grabbed his thick, scarred right hand. The skin across his knuckles was marred by white lines, callouses, and dark grease stains. The very hands that had rebuilt my crumbling bakery. The hands that had just ripped a rusted iron valve shut strictly to protect my inventory.

I lifted his massive hand to my mouth.

I pressed a slow, deliberate kiss to his rough knuckles.

Grady went perfectly still. His breathing hitched, stalling out in his wide chest.

I dragged my lips across the thick scar on his index finger. The taste of salt and copper touched my tongue. "You fix everything."

"Maisie." His voice dropped to a raw, dangerous gravel.

"I was terrified." I kept my grip tightly on his hand. I refused to let him pull away. "I was terrified that if I let you handle the heavy lifting, I would forget how to survive. I have survived on my own for ten years. But standing there, watching you put yourself between me and the freezing water... I do not want to survive anymore. I just want you to build the walls."

He ripped his hand from my grip.

Before I could register the loss, he grabbed my waist. His massive hands dug securely into my sides. He hauled me straight up from the floorboards, lifting me entirely off my feet. I gasped, grabbing his wide, wet shoulders for balance.

He stood up, carrying me with zero effort. He took two long strides and set me down on the dry, stainless steel prep table.

The cool metal bit through my damp jeans, but I barely noticed. Grady stepped perfectly between my parted thighs. He brought his dense, massive body flush against me, caging me completely against the edge of the counter.

He lifted his hands, tangling his rough fingers deep into my wet blonde hair. He tilted my head back.

"I am going to build walls so thick nothing ever touches you again," he vowed strictly. His dark eyes burned with absolute, unadulterated worship. "You are going to bake your pastries. You are going to stand behind this counter tomorrow and watch the entire town line up for your food. And when the pipes break, or the roof leaks, or the wind blows too hard, I will be the one standing in the water. Understood?"

"Understood." My lungs burned for air.

He brought his mouth down on mine.

The kiss was a total, aggressive consumption. He demanded absolute surrender, and I gave it to him instantly. I wrapped my arms securely around his thick neck, pulling his wet flannel directly against my cold sweater. The intense, searing heat of his mouth melted the freezing chill out of my bones.

He swept his tongue inside, tasting exactly like hot coffee and pure devotion. I met the driving stroke of his tongue with desperate hunger. He groaned, a deep, primal vibration rattling against my chest. He tightened his grip on my waist, dragging my hips flush against the apex of his thighs.

The blunt, rigid fact of his arousal pressed aggressively against my jeans.

I broke the kiss, gasping softly against his rough jaw. I dropped my hands to his wide chest, feeling the frantic, heavy thud of his heart beneath the thermal shirt.

"We have a massive puddle on the floor," I whispered, my voice incredibly shaky.

"I will dry the floor." He pressed an open-mouthed kiss below my ear, trailing hot, wet heat down the column of my neck. "I will dry the floor, I will secure the flour, and then I am going to strip you out of these wet clothes and warm you up until you cannot remember your own name."

"You are very demanding." I leaned my head back, giving him completely unrestricted access to my neck.

"I maintain the foundation." He bit gently at my collarbone, scraping his rough stubble against my sensitive skin.

He pulled back. The raw hunger in his eyes promised a total dismantling of my senses later tonight.

He stepped back from the counter, leaving me sitting safely on the dry steel. He walked back to the puddle. He dropped onto his knees and resumed wiping down the wet floorboards with the heavy shop towels. He worked with brutal, tireless stamina. His broad shoulders swayed with the repetitive, grueling motion.

I sat on the counter, swinging my boots slightly above the ground. I did not reach for a towel. I did not offer to help him wring out the dirty water.

I just watched him work.

The agonizing terror of failure was completely gone. The bakery was secure. The water was shut off. The heavy bags of premium flour sat perfectly dry on their wooden pallets.

Grady threw the soggy towels into a plastic bucket. He grabbed a dry rag and wiped the residual moisture from his massive hands. He looked up at me from the floor, his dark hair falling over his forehead. He did not look annoyed by the extra labor. He looked incredibly proud.

He had fixed the broken pipe. But more importantly, he had fixed me.

I smiled, a genuine, relaxed expression that felt entirely foreign on my face. I leaned back on my hands, completely at ease in the middle of a disaster zone. The safest place in the entire world was exactly right here, sitting quietly while a man in a heavy toolbelt handled the mess.

The mountain wind howled against the front glass, but inside the bakery, the foundation was perfectly solid.

Chapter Eleven

Devotion Under the Shop Lights

I wiped a smudge of powdered sugar from my cheek. My pulse drummed a frantic rhythm against my collarbone as Grady moved behind the display case. The roads had finally cleared. The morning sun glared off the towering snowdrifts outside, and the local vendors had piled into the bakery to inspect the ongoing renovations.

Grady was a mountain of a man. His broad, flannel-clad shoulders easily parted the sea of heavy winter coats and muddy boots. His calloused, scarred hands—the exact hands that had rebuilt my collapsing roof and gently carried me to bed when I passed out over my recipe books—were currently balancing a delicate tray of my fresh croissants.

A heavy, desperate heat pooled in my stomach, demanding I just let go. I wanted to sink into his quiet confidence. I wanted to finally drop the crushing mental load I had carried alone for my entire life.

But a stubborn, icy knot pulled tight against my ribs. If I leaned on him entirely, what happened to my armor? I had arrived in this snow-dusted town desperate to prove I could salvage this ruined building barehanded. Accepting his unconditional support was a dangerous surrender. If I completely trusted this massive contractor, I would be entirely defenseless.

Yet, as Grady caught my attention across the room, the hard planes of his face softening into absolute, unapologetic reverence, the frantic beating of my heart finally slowed. He stepped through the crowded space, completely oblivious to the watching locals. He was ready to show the entire town exactly whose ground he worshipped.

The heavy front glass door swung open, bringing a harsh draft of mountain air. Mr. Henderson, the local dairy and produce supplier, stomped his snow-covered boots onto the floor mat. He carried a thick clipboard stacked with invoices.

Henderson bypassed the front register entirely. He walked directly toward the center of the room, aiming straight for Grady.

"Morning, Grady." Henderson waved the clipboard in the air. "I brought the updated delivery schedules for the milk and butter. The storm messed up the routes. I need to know how you want to handle the loading dock freight."

A familiar, defensive posture locked my knees. I stiffened behind the pastry case. Contractors, suppliers, and bank managers always talked past me. They saw a petite, blonde baker covered in flour and instinctively searched the room for a man to give the final approval. I opened my mouth to intercept the supplier.

Grady beat me to it.

He lowered the tray of croissants onto the sturdy oak display counter. He did not take the clipboard. He turned his massive frame, completely blocking Henderson's path to the kitchen doors.

"I do not handle the freight schedule." His voice was a low, gravelly rumble that easily cut through the quiet chatter of the room.

"You are doing the build-out." Henderson pushed his clipboard forward, his brow furrowing. "You poured the concrete for the dock."

"I poured the concrete." Grady took a deliberate half-step forward. The impossible width of his chest swallowed the overhead light, casting a heavy shadow over the older supplier. "But I do not own the bakery. Maisie owns the building. Maisie signs the checks. Maisie dictates the delivery route."

Henderson blinked, taking a sudden step back from the massive contractor.

Grady hooked his scarred thumbs into his heavy leather toolbelt. He tilted his dark head toward the front counter. "You talk to the boss."

The entire room went perfectly silent.

The balance of power shifted completely beneath my boots. The defensive rigidity in my spine vanished. Henderson turned around, his posture immediately correcting into an apologetic hustle as he approached the display case.

"Miss Maisie," Henderson offered, placing the clipboard gently on the glass. "My apologies. Where do you want the heavy pallets dropped?"

"The back alley is cleared." I kept my voice steady, completely devoid of its usual frantic edge. "Drop the milk crates inside the secondary walk-in. I will sign the invoice now."

I scrawled my name across the paper. Henderson nodded respectfully, took his paperwork, and exited the shop.

I lifted my chin. Grady stood ten feet away. A dark amusement lit his harsh features. He did not demand praise. He did not flash a cocky grin to claim credit for defending my authority. He simply walked behind the counter, grabbed a clean glass, and filled it with ice water from the tap.

He crossed the floorboards. He stopped beside me and pressed the cold glass directly into my flour-dusted hand.

"Drink," he ordered softly.

"I am fine."

"You have been talking to vendors for three hours and you have not had a drop of water." He brushed a stray blonde curl behind my ear, his rough callouses catching slightly on my skin. "Drink the water, Maisie."

I brought the rim to my lips and drank. The cold water soothed my dry throat perfectly. He anticipated my physical needs before my brain even registered the thirst.

"Thank you," I whispered against the glass.

"I need to check the plumbing on the utility sink." He dropped his gaze to my mouth. "Go inventory the dry goods. We open tomorrow."

He turned and vanished into the back prep room.

I set the empty glass on the counter. The dry goods inventory. The task loomed over my head like a dark storm cloud. The delivery truck had dropped off six eighty-pound burlap sacks of premium bread flour yesterday. They were currently sitting on a wooden pallet in the center of the pantry. I needed to manually drag them onto the heavy-duty metal shelves and rotate the older stock to the front.

My lower back throbbed in preemptive agony. Moving four hundred and eighty pounds of dead weight was going to destroy my arms, but I could not afford to pay a stock boy.

I grabbed my inventory clipboard. I walked through the swinging wooden doors into the back kitchen. The scent of sawdust and burnt sugar hung thick in the air.

I reached the pantry and pulled the heavy door open.

I froze on the threshold.

The wooden delivery pallet was completely empty.

I lifted my head. The massive burlap sacks of flour were perfectly stacked on the reinforced lower shelves. Every single bag was meticulously aligned. The older inventory from last month had been shifted neatly to the front, the expiration dates facing outward for easy reading. The sugar bins were topped off. The heavy gallon jugs of vanilla extract were lined up like soldiers on the middle tier.

The clipboard slipped from my fingers. It clattered loudly against the floorboards.

The heavy, rusted armor I had worn for ten years cracked straight down the middle. My shoulders dropped a full two inches. The tight, agonizing coil in my lower spine unraveled completely. I did not have to brace my body for the grueling physical labor. I did not have to calculate the rotation schedule. He had completely eliminated the problem before I even touched the doorknob.

The crushing mental load physically evaporated from my lungs. A shaky, desperate sound scraped its way up my throat.

A loud thud echoed from the utility sink across the room.

Grady stood near the mop buckets. He tossed a dirty, grease-stained rag into a red plastic bin. He turned away from the rusted plumbing fixture. He stopped, taking in my frozen posture in the pantry doorway.

He abandoned his tools instantly. He crossed the floorboards with heavy, deliberate strides, his steel-toed boots striking the wood like a drumbeat. He stepped directly into the narrow space behind the prep counter, forcing me backward until my spine hit the metal shelving. He boxed me in completely.

He planted his thick thighs on either side of my knees. He rested his massive hands on the shelving on either side of my head, trapping me in a cage of solid muscle and dark flannel.

The balance of power shifted slightly beneath my boots. I tipped my chin up, meeting his burning gaze.

"You rotated my entire inventory." I grabbed the front of his shirt, my voice a breathless rasp.

"I did."

"Those flour sacks weigh eighty pounds each."

"They do." He leaned closer. The intense heat radiating from his broad chest wrapped around me, a physical shield against the cold mountain draft. "And you weigh slightly more than one of them. You have no business hauling that freight."

"I am the business owner. I am supposed to handle the stock." I pressed my palms flat against the unyielding muscle of his abdomen. "You are spoiling me, Grady. You are stripping away every single task I have. What am I supposed to do if you handle everything?"

"You are supposed to bake." He dropped his right hand from the shelf. He cupped my jaw, his thumb scraping gently across my cheekbone. "You are the boss out there, Maisie. I made sure every vendor in this town knows it. But in here?"

He stepped a fraction of an inch closer, his denim-clad thighs brushing aggressively against mine.

"In here, you belong to me. You let me carry the weight. You let me pull the heavy shifts." His voice dropped an entire octave, morphing into a raw, territorial growl. "I will haul every grain of sugar into this building until my back gives out, as long as you promise to stop fighting me and just let me take care of you."

The last defensive posture in my body collapsed. I did not want to fight him anymore. The struggle was over.

I slid my hands up his chest, tangling my fingers into the collar of his thermal shirt. I pulled his face down.

He met me halfway, bringing his mouth down on mine with devastating, bruising force. He kissed me like a starving man. His lips were rough, demanding absolute surrender. I opened for him instantly. He swept his hot, commanding tongue inside, tasting exactly like dark roast coffee and pure devotion.

I poured every ounce of my relief right back into him, meeting his aggressive rhythm. He groaned, a deep vibration rattling against my chest. He slid his massive arms around my waist, lifting my feet completely off the floorboards.

He pinned me securely against the metal rack, his thick waist pressing hard against my stomach. The blunt, heavy ridge of his arousal pushed through the thick denim of his jeans, pressing an unmistakable demand against my hips.

"You are so damn capable," I gasped against his lips, breaking the kiss just enough to drag oxygen into my burning lungs.

"I am thorough." He kissed the sensitive skin just below my ear, his dark stubble scratching delightfully against my neck. "They love your food out there, Maisie. I watched them clear out the display case in three hours. I told you they would."

"They showed up because you fixed the roof."

"They showed up because you are brilliant." He set me down slowly, letting my boots touch the solid floorboards. He kept his hands firmly anchored on my hips. "I just built the box. You are the one putting the magic inside it."

He stepped back, giving me exactly enough room to breathe. He reached down and picked up my fallen clipboard from the floor. He handed it back to me.

"The inventory is logged." He tapped his scarred finger against the metal clip. "Check the numbers. Then go sit by the stove and rest your feet."

I took the clipboard. The numbers were perfectly tallied in his sharp, architectural handwriting.

Grady turned his back, returning to his heavy steel toolbox near the utility sink. He picked up his wrench. He did not ask for a single favor in return. He simply resumed his grueling physical labor, a silent guardian in a sawdust-covered shirt.

I held the clipboard tight to my chest. The afternoon sun broke through the high frosted windows, catching the light dusting of flour in the air and casting warm shadows across the freshly swept floorboards.

Chapter Twelve

BUILT TO YIELD

The scent of fresh sawdust, dark roast coffee, and burnt sugar hung heavy in the quiet air of the bakery. The evening sun had dipped behind the snow-capped mountain peaks, leaving the shop floor bathed in the warm, artificial glow of the overhead track lights.

I stood completely still by the stainless steel prep station. My apron was covered in white flour, and my lower back carried a familiar, dull ache from twelve solid hours of recipe testing. I should have been washing the heavy mixing bowls. I should have been tallying the final inventory numbers on my clipboard before tomorrow's grand opening.

Instead, I watched Grady work.

He was on his hands and knees in the center of the room, securing the massive oak display counter to the floorboards. The faded, grease-stained denim of his work jeans stretched punishingly tight across his thick, powerful thighs. He shifted his weight, and his dark grey thermal shirt clung to his expansive back, defining the heavy, brutal slabs of muscle flexing with every aggressive turn of his steel wrench. A heavy bead of sweat rolled down the thick column of his neck, disappearing into his collar. His massive, calloused hands gripped the heavy metal tool with total, uncompromising authority. He was a mountain of rough-hewn capability. Watching those dirty, scarred hands master the physical world created a reckless, pooling heat right behind my ribs. I wanted those massive hands on me. I wanted his heavy, exhausted body to completely flatten my remaining defenses.

The heavy steel wrench clattered against the floorboards.

Grady sat back on his heavy heels. He wiped the sweat from his forehead with the back of his thick forearm, leaving a faint streak of dark grease across his skin. He turned his head slowly.

He caught me staring.

A dark amusement lit his harsh, masculine features. He did not rush to stand up. He stayed perfectly grounded, letting his intense gaze drag deliberately from the toes of my flour-dusted boots up to the messy bun sitting on top of my head.

"The bolts are secure." His gravelly voice easily cut through the quiet room.

"I am inspecting the structural integrity." I crossed my arms, lifting my chin to challenge him. The old, frantic anxiety that usually dictated my every move was completely absent. A new, unfamiliar confidence took its place. "You are bolting down my premium oak counter. I require perfection."

"I use a heavy-duty level." He picked up the wrench and tossed it effortlessly into the steel toolbox sitting nearby. The metal clasps snapped shut with a sharp crack.

"You use a lot of things." I took a deliberate step forward, leaving the safety of the prep station. "But I am the business owner. I am the one who gives the final approval."

Grady went perfectly still. The amusement vanished from his face, instantly replaced by a dangerous, predatory focus. The muscle in his square jaw feathered.

He stood up.

The impossible width of his shoulders completely eclipsed the overhead lights. He crossed the freshly swept floorboards with long, heavy strides. His steel-toed boots thudded against the wood in a relentless rhythm. The air in the room suddenly felt incredibly thin. The balance of power shifted completely beneath my boots, but I refused to take a single step backward.

He stopped exactly one foot away from me. The radiant heat coming off his massive body wrapped around my petite frame. He smelled like cut pine, motor oil, and pure, unadulterated man.

He reached down. He hooked his large thumbs into the heavy leather loops of his toolbelt, unbuckled the brass clasp, and let the heavy rig drop to the floor. It hit the wood with a massive thud.

"You give the final approval on the pastries." He lifted his right hand, brushing a rough knuckle against the sensitive skin of my throat. My pulse drummed a frantic rhythm against my collarbone. "I give the final approval on everything else. Including exactly what time you stop working."

"You do not dictate my schedule, Grady."

"I dictate your health." He stepped closer, eliminating the space between us entirely. His thick thighs boxed me in. "You have been on your feet since dawn. You are completely exhausted, and your hands are shaking."

"I am fine."

"You are stubborn."

Before I could formulate a sharp reply, he dropped his hands to my waist. His massive, scarred fingers dug securely into my sides. He hauled me straight up from the floorboards, lifting my entire body into the air with zero effort. A sharp gasp tore out of my throat. I grabbed his wide, solid shoulders for balance.

He took two strides and sat me down directly onto the sturdy surface of the newly bolted oak display counter.

The polished wood felt cool through my denim jeans. The counter did not shift a single millimeter under the sudden weight. He had anchored it perfectly.

Grady stepped directly between my parted thighs. He pressed his dense, unyielding body flush against the edge of the wood, caging me completely.

For my entire life, I have been the one holding up the collapsing roof. I am so used to carrying the weight of the world on my own exhausted shoulders that the idea of surrender feels like a terrifying free-fall. Looking up at Grady now—massive, broad-shouldered, completely eclipsing the dim light of the bakery—panic flutters in my chest, tight and breathless. It is not just his crushing physical size that scares me, though the reality of my petite frame taking him is daunting enough. It is what this vulnerability means.

If I let him do this, if I let him inside, I am finally dropping the solitary armor I have worn since the day I arrived in this mountain town.

But then his rough, calloused hands frame my face. Hands that rebuilt my shattered bakery, hands that carried me to bed when I was too tired to stand. He looks at me like I am the most precious thing he has ever held, demanding absolutely nothing in return.

The fear melts into a desperate, aching desire. I do not want to be strong anymore. I want to be dismantled by him. I part my thighs further, craving the beautiful, terrifying weight of him finally sinking into me.

"Do it," I whispered. My voice cracked perfectly down the middle.

"Are you sure?" He dragged his thumbs across my cheekbones, his dark eyes burning with absolute worship. "Once I start, Maisie, I am not going to stop. I am going to completely tear down every single wall you have left."

"Tear them down."

He brought his mouth down on mine.

The kiss was a total consumption. He did not ask for permission; he claimed it. His hot, rough lips demanded absolute surrender, and I opened for him instantly. He swept his tongue inside, tasting exactly like dark coffee and relentless devotion. I tangled my fingers into his thick, dark hair, anchoring myself to him as the world spun completely off its axis.

He broke the kiss just enough to drag oxygen into his lungs. He dropped his massive hands to the hem of my flour-dusted apron. He untied the strings with rapid, uncompromising efficiency. He pulled the fabric over my head and tossed it onto the floorboards.

My thin cotton sweater followed a second later.

The cool air of the shop bit into my bare skin, but the intense heat radiating from his broad chest immediately fought back the chill. I sat before him in nothing but my bra and jeans.

Grady did not rush. He treated my body with the exact same meticulous, obsessive care he used to frame a load-bearing wall. He traced the soft curve of my collarbone with his scarred index finger. The rough, blistering friction of his working man's callouses against my delicate skin sent a heavy jolt straight to my core.

He unclasped my bra. The garment fell away.

His breathing stalled out completely in his wide chest. He stared at my bare breasts, his jaw clenched so incredibly tight I thought his teeth might shatter.

"Perfect," he growled.

He leaned down. He dragged his hot, open mouth over the peak of my breast. He pulled the tight bud between his lips, applying a steady, rhythmic suction that forced a loud, ragged moan right out of my throat. My spine bowed off the wood. I gripped the edge of the oak counter helplessly.

He worked his way down my body, his dark scruff scratching delightfully against my sensitive stomach. He gripped the brass zipper of my jeans. He ripped it down in one smooth, aggressive motion. He hooked his thick thumbs into the waistband and dragged the denim entirely off my legs, taking my socks with them.

I sat completely naked on the display counter.

"Your turn," I demanded softly. My hands shook as I reached for the hem of his thermal shirt.

He obliged instantly. He grabbed the dark fabric and pulled it over his head, discarding it onto the pile of clothing on the floorboards.

The absolute width of his bare chest stole the oxygen totally from my lungs. Thick cords of muscle stood out on his shoulders and abdomen. Jagged, pale white scars from years of manual labor tracked across his ribs and left bicep. He was a machine built for grueling physical endurance.

He reached down and unfastened his heavy work jeans. He pushed the denim and his thick cotton underwear down his thighs, kicking them away.

The blunt, rigid fact of his erection sprang totally free.

He was staggeringly massive. Thick, heavily veined, and completely terrifying in his dimensions. A cold sweat broke across the back of my neck. My petite frame was absolutely dwarfed by the sheer reality of his body.

He noticed my hesitation immediately. He stepped closer, fitting his thick waist right between my parted knees. He rested his large, warm hands on my bare thighs.

"Look at me, Maisie," he ordered softly.

I dragged my gaze up from his waist, meeting his steady stare.

"I am big," he stated calmly. "But I know exactly how to handle you. I am never going to hurt you. Do you trust me?"

"I trust you." The words were an absolute truth. "But I need you to go slow."

"I am going to take all night."

He dropped to his knees on the floorboards.

The sudden change in elevation put his face perfectly level with my center. He parted my thighs wider, opening me completely to the cool air of the shop. He did not hesitate. He buried his face directly against my wetness.

His tongue darted out, dragging a long, deliberate stripe straight up my slick core.

I cried out, my fingers instantly digging into his bare, muscular shoulders.

He settled into the work. He lapped at my folds, drinking my sweet taste with aggressive, starving enthusiasm. He parted my petals with his scarred thumbs, exposing the ultra-sensitive bundle of nerves. He wrapped his hot lips around my clitoris, applying a firm, steady suction that made my hips buck violently off the wood.

"Grady!"

"I have you." He spoke the words directly against my damp flesh.

He lifted his right hand. Two thick, calloused fingers slid over my drenched entrance. He pressed forward, stretching me completely open. His digits filled me tight, simulating the agonizing stretch I was about to endure. He pumped his hand in tandem with his devouring mouth, creating an overwhelming, intoxicating friction.

My internal muscles clamped down hard around his fingers. The raw anticipation built into a blinding, white-hot pressure.

"That is it," he praised, his voice a rough vibration against my skin. "Open up for me. Get completely ready."

He drove his fingers deeper, striking a deep, aching spot inside me. I shattered. A violent climax ripped through my petite frame. I screamed his name into the empty bakery. My legs shook entirely out of control.

Grady stayed totally anchored between my thighs, drinking every single drop of my release. He swallowed my broken sounds until the violent tremors wracking my body finally faded.

He slowly pulled his fingers free. He stood up in one fluid, powerful surge.

My chest heaved. I was completely unraveled, thoroughly melted into a puddle of compliant heat.

Grady gripped my hips. He pulled my body forward until my rear was positioned perfectly at the edge of the oak counter. He stepped squarely into the gap. The thick, blunt head of his arousal traced the wet, slick entrance to my body.

The searing heat of his skin burned against mine.

"Wrap your legs around me," he commanded.

I lifted my trembling legs, hooking my ankles securely behind his thick waist.

He rested his massive hands flat on the wooden counter on either side of my hips, bracing his heavy weight. He looked down at me, his jaw set in stone. He pushed forward, breaching my entrance with the blunt crown.

The stretch was absolute. A sharp gasp tore out of my mouth.

"Look at me," he demanded roughly.

I forced my eyes open.

"You take me so well." He pushed forward another agonizing inch. The thick girth of him stretched my internal walls completely taut. "So damn sweet, Maisie."

My fingernails bit into the solid muscle of his forearms. I tried to adjust, my hips tilting upward to accommodate his staggering size.

He stopped completely. He held perfectly still, burying exactly half his length inside me. The pressure was a heavy, burning ache that bordered directly on total panic.

"Breathe," he ordered. He leaned down, pressing an open-mouthed kiss to the pulse point jumping frantically at my neck. "Let your body adjust. I am not moving until you tell me to."

The total control he exercised over his own driving need stripped away the last ounce of my fear. Even absolutely buried inside me, fighting his instinct to thrust, he prioritized my comfort over his release.

I let the tension bleed entirely out of my spine. I relaxed my inner muscles, letting the slick heat of my body mold perfectly around his thick invasion. The burning stretch slowly morphed into a deep, desperate fullness.

"More," I whispered against his shoulder.

A ragged groan ripped out of his throat.

He gripped my hips with his large, calloused hands. He anchored me completely against the wood. With one slow, devastating thrust, he drove his hips completely forward, sinking to the hilt.

The physical impact knocked the breath cleanly out of my lungs. I was entirely full. The overwhelming reality of his size completely overwhelmed my senses.

"Good girl," he praised, his voice fracturing. "You are so perfect."

He slowly pulled back. He dragged almost his entire length out of my body, leaving only the thick crown inside. Then, he drove forward again, burying himself completely to the hilt.

The blunt intrusion hit exactly the deepest, most sensitive spot inside me. I threw my head back, a loud, broken moan echoing off the drywall.

Grady established a slow, grinding rhythm. He did not pound into me with reckless abandon. He drove his hips with deliberate, uncompromising stamina, making sure every single thrust stretched me completely open. The heavy oak counter absorbed the brutal force of our bodies without a single creak. He had built the foundation perfectly.

"You belong to me now," he growled, entirely losing his grip on his restraint. He pumped his hips faster, the wet slap of his thighs hitting mine echoing like gunshots in the quiet room.

"Yes." I dug my nails into his wide back, anchoring myself to the solid mountain of his body. "Grady, please."

"I have you." He reached down, slipping his thick thumb between our joined bodies. He pressed hard against my swollen clitoris, trapping the nerve directly beneath his rough callous as he drove his hips deep.

The dual friction completely obliterated my mind. The world narrowed down entirely to the brutal heat of his body and the punishing, perfect rhythm of his thrusts.

"Give it to me," he demanded, his breathing heavy and erratic. "Let go!"

The blinding climax hit me like a freight train.

A ragged scream tore out of my throat. My internal walls clamped down violently around his thick length, milking his rigid flesh as wave after wave of absolute pleasure crashed over my overworked body.

Grady shouted my name, a rough, primal sound that rattled the tools on the nearby benches. He drove his hips forward one final, devastating time, completely burying himself to the hilt. His massive frame went totally rigid. Hot, heavy fluid flooded deep inside my womb, pulsing in time with his racing heartbeat.

He collapsed forward.

His broad, heavy chest landed flush against mine. He rested his forehead in the crook of my neck, his lungs dragging in massive, jagged breaths. His heavy weight pressed me entirely into the solid wood counter.

I did not attempt to push him off. I wrapped my arms securely around his wide shoulders, holding him exactly where he was. The agonizing terror of failing alone was completely gone, systematically deconstructed by the man currently pinning me to the wood.

He slowly lifted his head. His dark hair was utterly disheveled, falling across his damp forehead.

He pulled out of my body, the slick slide causing a final, delightful twitch in my lower stomach. He did not step away. He reached out, his incredibly gentle hands brushing a stray blonde curl from my cheek.

"You built a good counter," I whispered, my voice completely shot.

A dark amusement lit his harsh features. "I build things to last."

He stepped back just enough to grab his discarded dark grey thermal shirt from the floor. He shook the dust off the fabric. Instead of putting it back on his massive frame, he carefully pulled the soft cotton over my head, completely swaddling my bare torso in his scent.

"I need to clean up the shop," I protested softly, though I made absolutely no move to slide off the wood.

"You are done for the night." He grabbed his work jeans, stepping easily into the heavy denim. He fastened the brass button. "I will sweep the floorboards. I will lock the doors. And then I am carrying you upstairs to bed."

I watched him walk toward the utility closet to grab the broom. The heavy tread of his steel-toed boots crushed a few scattered wood shavings into the floor. The bakery was perfectly quiet, the foundation completely secure.

I pulled the collar of his thermal shirt securely under my chin. I rested my hands on the solid oak counter, letting the deep, overwhelming wave of absolute security wash over me completely.

Chapter Thirteen

Warm Water and Quiet Praise

Adrenaline thrummed in my veins as I stood beside the narrow bed. The small apartment above the bakery was quiet. Maisie rested deep in the tangled white sheets. Her petite blonde head barely made a dent in the pillows. A sharp, clawing tension gripped my throat. I stared at my scarred, calloused hands. These rough palms were built for swinging a framing hammer and hauling eighty-pound bags of concrete. The massive reality of my size compared to her delicate frame made my chest tight. A cold sweat broke across the back of my neck. What if I had broken her?

I had tried to be careful downstairs on the counter. I treated her with absolute, unwavering caution. But the memory of burying myself entirely inside her, the brutal stretch of her taking my full weight, played on a loop in my mind.

Yet, she had not broken. She had arched beneath me, fiercely demanding every ounce of my strength. She shattered my restraint until all I could do was worship the ground she walked on. The desire to keep her—to build a fortress around this exhausted, stubbornly independent woman and never let the world touch her again—was a living, breathing ache inside my ribs.

She had spent her entire life carrying the weight of the world alone. Even tonight, she tried to maintain control, until I physically loved the burden out of her. Now, her breathing was finally even. No collapsing bakery roofs. No failing pipes. Just Maisie.

Turning away from the mattress, I headed toward the bathroom. My steel-toed boots thudded softly against the worn floorboards. Warm water spilled into the porcelain sink as I twisted the brass faucet. After testing the temperature with my knuckles, I grabbed a soft white washcloth and soaked it through. I wrung out the excess moisture. Setting the cloth aside, I filled a clean glass from the tap.

If she woke up sticky and uncomfortable, she would immediately try to handle it herself. She would push out of bed and march to the shower on exhausted legs. I refused to let her lift a single finger.

The bedroom remained perfectly quiet when I returned. I set the glass on the night-stand, then lowered myself onto the edge of the mattress. The old metal springs groaned under my weight.

Maisie shifted. Her eyelashes fluttered apart. She looked up at me, blinking against the dim light filtering through the frosted window.

"Grady." Her voice was a soft, gravelly rasp.

"Do not move." I pulled the white sheet back, exposing her bare legs to the cool air.

I brought the warm, damp cloth to her inner thighs. I wiped away the slick evidence of our time downstairs. The heated cotton glided smoothly over her sensitive skin. I moved with absolute, terrifying caution, treating her body with more reverence than a delicate stained-glass installation.

She lifted her head off the pillow. She reached out, her small fingers wrapping around my thick wrist. "I can do that."

"I know you can." I did not drop the cloth. I easily overpowered her grip, pinning her hand gently to the mattress. "But you do not have to. I am taking care of it."

A stubborn flush rose on her cheeks. "You are going to spoil me."

"That is the entire point." I finished cleaning her. I tossed the washcloth onto the floor near my boots. Reaching for the glass of water, I brought the rim to her lips. "Drink."

She obeyed. She took three long swallows, her throat working rhythmically. I pulled the glass away and set it down.

Maisie did not retreat under the covers. She pushed herself up onto her elbows. Her gaze dragged deliberately from my bare chest down to the worn work jeans I had pulled back on downstairs.

"You are sitting in my bed wearing dirty denim." She tilted her chin. The frantic pacing that usually governed her every move was entirely gone. In its place, a new, fiery confidence bloomed.

A dark amusement lit my face. "I was working."

"The work is done." She shifted her knees, moving closer to the edge of the mattress. Her bare breasts brushed against my forearm. A massive jolt of heat slammed directly into my core.

"There is always more to build." I stayed perfectly still, letting her test the boundaries.

She reached out. Her small hands found the brass button of my jeans. "Take these off. You are scratching my sheets."

My jaw clenched. The restraint I had meticulously rebuilt over the last twenty minutes fractured instantly. I stood up from the mattress. I unfastened the button and ripped the zipper down in one aggressive motion. I kicked my boots off, letting them hit the wall with a loud thud. The worn denim and my underwear followed a second later.

I was completely bare. The blunt, rigid fact of my arousal sprang fully to life, pointing directly at her.

She looked at the immense width of my chest, tracking the pale scars over my ribs, before her gaze dropped entirely. Her lungs burned for air. The overwhelming reality of my dimensions in the small, intimate space of her bedroom was intense. But she did not flinch. She refused to look away.

"Come here," she demanded softly.

I climbed onto the mattress. The wooden frame shrieked in protest as my knees hit the covers. I crawled over her, caging her petite form completely beneath my massive body. I braced my weight on my forearms, refusing to crush her.

"Are you sore?" I brushed my thumb over her lower lip.

"I am ready." Her fingers tangled into my dark hair. She pulled my mouth down to hers.

The kiss was a total, consuming fire. I swept my tongue inside, tasting the remnants of the water she just drank. She opened for me willingly, meeting my dominant rhythm with desperate hunger. I dragged my mouth down her jaw, pressing an open-mouthed kiss to the jumping pulse at her throat.

Shifting my hips, I wedged my thick thighs directly between hers. She parted her legs wide, offering me unrestricted access. I reached down. My calloused fingers found her slick entrance. She was already dripping wet, her body perfectly primed.

"You feel so good." I rubbed my thumb over her swollen clitoris.

A ragged moan tore out of her throat. Her hips bucked upward, chasing the friction.

I guided the blunt crown of my arousal against her opening. I did not rush. I held my torso rigid, my muscles burning with the effort to maintain absolute control. I pressed forward, breaching her entrance.

The stretch was agonizingly sweet. Her internal walls were incredibly tight, gripping my flesh with blinding heat. I sank a single inch inside.

"Look at me." My voice dropped to a raw gravel.

Maisie opened her eyes. The blue irises were blown wide, dark with unadulterated need.

"Tell me what you want." I held perfectly still, grinding my teeth against the brutal urge to bury myself to the hilt.

"All of it." Her nails dug into the solid muscle of my back. "Do not hold back, Grady. Please."

I let my restraint snap. I drove my hips forward in one slow, devastating thrust, burying myself entirely inside her.

The physical impact knocked the breath cleanly out of my lungs. I was full. The tight, slick heat of her body clamped around my thick length, milking me with every frantic beat of her heart.

"Good girl," I praised roughly. "You take me so well."

"Grady." My name was a fractured plea on her lips.

I established a deep, punishing rhythm. Pulling almost entirely out, I let the cool air brush my skin before driving forward to the hilt. The iron bedframe banged aggressively against the drywall. I did not care. The entire world narrowed down to the woman writhing beneath me.

I drove my hips harder. The wet slap of my flesh against hers echoed in the small room. She wrapped her long legs around my waist, locking her ankles over the small of my back to anchor me deep. The new angle granted me even further access. I struck the deepest, most sensitive spot inside her womb.

She threw her head back. Her teeth bared.

"That is it," I growled, maintaining the brutal pace. "Give it to me, Maisie. Let go."

I slipped my hand between our joined bodies. Finding the swollen bundle of sensitive nerves, I clamped my rough thumb down exactly as I thrust forward.

The dual friction destroyed her control. A violent, blinding climax ripped through her petite frame. She screamed my name, her nails leaving half-moon indentations across my wide shoulders. Her internal muscles clamped down hard, wringing every ounce of sanity from my brain.

I drove forward one final time. I buried myself as deep as physically possible and let go. Hot fluid flooded her, pulsing in time with my racing heartbeat. A ragged shout tore out of my throat.

My arms gave out. I collapsed forward, dropping my weight onto the mattress beside her. I pulled her flush against my side, tucking her head under my chin. My lungs dragged in massive, jagged breaths.

We lay in the dark for a long time. The sweat cooled on my skin. Maisie's breathing shifted into the slow, rhythmic cadence of deep sleep. She curled her small hand against my pectoral muscle.

I did not close my eyes. My body was exhausted, but my mind raced with logistics.

The grand opening was exactly six hours away. The display cases were bolted down. The plumbing was secure. But the commercial kitchen required a massive amount of prep work before the sun rose.

I waited until I was absolutely certain she was asleep. I carefully unhooked her arm from my chest. Rolling off the mattress, my bare feet hit the cold floorboards. I picked up my cast-off jeans from the corner. I stepped into the worn denim, pulling the zipper up. I grabbed my dark grey thermal shirt and pulled it over my head.

I looked back at the bed. Maisie looked incredibly small surrounded by the white sheets. For ten years, she had fought every battle alone. She had measured every ounce of flour, fixed every broken machine, and carried the agonizing terror of failure completely by herself.

Never again.

I walked out of the bedroom. I crept down the wooden stairs, avoiding the creaky third step. I hit the landing and pushed through the solid door into the bakery.

The shop was dark, illuminated only by the faint glow of the streetlamps cutting through the frosted front windows. The scent of pine wood and burnt sugar hit my lungs. I walked behind the newly installed oak counter. I flicked the circuit breaker for the kitchen.

The harsh overhead track lights hummed to life.

The commercial space was a disaster zone. Metal mixing bowls sat unwashed in the sinks. Flour coated the stainless steel prep tables in white layers. Baking sheets were piled haphazardly near the ovens.

If Maisie woke up to this mess, the pacing would return. The heavy burden would settle right back onto her delicate shoulders.

I rolled my sleeves past my elbows. I grabbed a large plastic bucket, a stiff scrub brush, and a gallon of industrial degreaser from the utility closet.

The massive commercial dishwasher roared to life, generating a thick cloud of hot steam. I loaded the dirty metal bowls into the plastic racks. The repetitive, physical labor grounded me. My scarred hands moved with relentless efficiency, scraping dried dough off the wire whisks. I sanitized the stainless steel tables, wiping them down until the metal gleamed under the track lights. I reorganized the pantry shelves, double-checking the expiration dates on the dairy deliveries.

Two hours later, the dishwashing station was bone dry and organized.

I grabbed a wide push broom. I swept the pressure-treated floorboards, collecting every stray wood shaving and dropped crumb into a neat pile. I dumped the debris into the trash bin.

Crossing to the massive baking ovens, I checked the gas lines. The brass fittings I had installed the previous week held perfectly tight. A quick twist ignited the pilot lights. The blue flames flared, bringing the internal temperature up to a precise three hundred and fifty degrees. I recalibrated the thermostats, guaranteeing an absolutely even bake for her delicate pastries.

The fight for her independence was dissolving entirely. I did not want to control her vision. I only wanted to amplify her success.

I walked to the coffee station. I ground a pound of premium dark roast beans. I set the metal filter into the machine and primed the water reservoir. I left the power switch in the off position, ready to be flipped the second she walked downstairs.

The kitchen was spotless.

The eastern horizon outside the frosted windows began to crack with the first pale light of morning. The snow-covered mountain town was waking up. In a few hours, a line of locals would wrap around the entire block. They would eat her food, and they would realize exactly how brilliant she was.

I grabbed a clean white towel and wiped the grease from my knuckles. I tossed the rag onto the counter.

I walked back upstairs. The door to the apartment was cracked open. I stepped quietly into the bedroom.

Maisie remained asleep. The blankets had slipped down, exposing her smooth, bare shoulder to the cool morning air. I walked to the edge of the mattress. I reached down, pulling the thick duvet up, tucking it securely beneath her chin.

I leaned over and kissed the top of her blonde head.

"I built the box." I whispered into the quiet room. "Now you bake the bread."

The winter sun broke over the mountain peaks, flooding the room in bright, golden light.

Chapter Fourteen

Blueprints on the Workbench

The red ink bled into the cheap paper of the ledger, a stark and final line drawn straight through the words *Pastel Rose Ceramic Backsplash*.

I pressed the cap back onto the pen with a sharp click. The bare bulb suspended above the folding table cast harsh shadows over the numbers, illuminating exactly how thin my margins had become. The upgraded commercial ovens had eaten the contingency fund. The emergency plumbing repair had swallowed the rest. If I wanted to open the doors by the end of the week, sacrifices had to be made.

Glossy white paint would have to do. It was sanitary. It was cheap. But a dull, familiar ache throbbed right behind my ribs as I stared at the crossed-out line. Those tiles had been the anchor of my design, the single splash of warmth in a stainless-steel commercial kitchen.

Across the room, the high-pitched whine of a power drill cut out abruptly.

Grady lowered the tool, blowing a thin layer of sawdust off the freshly hung pantry door. He wore a faded grey thermal shirt pushed up to his elbows, exposing forearms corded with thick muscle and tracked with pale, jagged scars. Turning away from the fitted hinges, he crossed the room toward me. Wood shavings crunched softly beneath his steel-toed boots.

He stopped at the edge of the folding table. The radiant heat coming off his broad chest fought back the persistent chill of the drafty room. He leaned over, planting his calloused knuckles on the surface of the table, and studied the open ledger.

"What are we crossing out?"

"The backsplash." I slid the notebook an inch closer to my chest, an instinctive, defensive shield. "The tile quote came back too high. I am reallocating the funds to cover the first delivery of wholesale butter and cream."

Grady kept his gaze locked on the paper. A muscle feathered in his square jaw. "You spent four weeks picking out that exact shade of pink."

"And now I am picking out a bucket of waterproof white paint." I forced a pragmatic, breezy tone, refusing to let him see the disappointment clawing at my throat. "It is fine, Grady. The customers are going to look at the pastries in the display case, not the wall behind the grease traps."

He finally looked up. His dark eyes studied my face, systematically dismantling the casual mask I tried to wear. He did not offer empty platitudes. He did not suggest we run the numbers again or take out another line of credit.

He just nodded once, stood up straight, and walked toward the kitchen's back exit.

The heavy metal door groaned open, letting a vicious gust of mountain wind and swirling snow bite into the warm bakery. Grady stepped out into the alley, leaving the door cracked behind him.

My lungs tightened. I stood up from the folding stool, abandoning the ledger. The wind howled through the gap in the door frame, bringing the sharp scent of pine and exhaust. A minute later, the crunch of boots on the icy pavement grew louder.

Grady shoved the door wide open with his hip.

He carried three thick, water-stained cardboard boxes stacked precariously against his chest. The dense weight of the load was obvious in the rigid strain of his shoulders, but he carried them with brutal, uncompromising ease. Kicking the door shut behind him, he hauled the load directly into the center of the kitchen and dropped them onto the floorboards with a resounding thud.

Dust plumed into the air.

"What is this?" I stepped around the prep counter.

Kneeling beside the stack, Grady hooked his scarred index finger under the packing tape of the top box and ripped the cardboard open. He reached inside, pulling out a six-by-six ceramic square.

The overhead lights caught the gleaming, high-end glaze. It was a perfect, delicate shade of pastel pink.

The air rushed out of me in a fractured gasp.

"A tech executive from the city built a sprawling summer house up the ridge last spring," Grady explained, his gravelly voice echoing in the quiet room. He ran his rough thumb over the pristine, fragile surface of the tile. "His wife special-ordered three pallets of this exact ceramic for their master bath. The day I went to install it, she changed her mind. Said the tone was too warm. They told the crew to haul it to the county dump."

I stared at the ceramic, my mind struggling to process the impossible stroke of luck. "And you kept them?"

"I loaded them into the back of my truck and stacked them in the corner of my workshop." He set the tile carefully on the counter. "Figured someone would want them eventually. Turns out, I was saving them for you."

The tight, agonizing coil in my lower spine began to unravel. For a decade, every single obstacle in my life had required grueling, solitary sacrifice. If the car broke down, I walked. If a bill ran high, I starved. But standing in the center of the bakery, watching this man pull premium building materials out of thin air simply to protect my vision, the defensive armor I kept strapped to my ribs cracked straight down the middle.

"Grady, these are premium tiles." My voice shook. "I cannot afford to buy these from you."

"You are not buying anything." He stood up, towering over the boxes. "They have been collecting dust for eight months. They belong on your wall."

"I cannot just take them."

"Yes, you can." He closed the distance between us in two long strides. Framing my face with his large, rough hands, he tilted my chin up. The blistering friction of his working-man's callouses against my skin sent a deep, reckless heat straight to my core. "You are going to stop fighting me, Maisie. I am not a bank. I am not a vendor. You do not owe me a damn spreadsheet for this."

"I am used to paying my own way."

"I know." His thumbs swept gently across my cheekbones. "But you do not have to anymore. Just say thank you, and go sit by the stove while I mix the mortar."

My throat tightened painfully. The fierce, stubborn pride that had kept me alive for so long dissolved under the sheer weight of his devotion. I did not want to push him away. I wanted to sink into the unyielding fortress he was building around me.

"Thank you." I whispered the words against his palm.

A dark amusement lit his harsh features. "You are very welcome."

He dropped his hands, turning his focus immediately to the physical labor. Retrieving a large plastic bucket and a steel mixing paddle from his supply corner, he filled the container with dry, grey thin-set powder. He added water from the utility sink, attaching the paddle to his power drill. The aggressive, grating roar of the spinning metal chewing through the wet clay filled the commercial kitchen.

I did not go sit by the woodstove in the apartment upstairs. I stayed exactly where I was, leaning my hip against the stainless steel prep table, watching him work.

The frantic anxiety of the impending grand opening faded into a quiet, profound stillness.

Grady slapped a thick, wet layer of mortar onto the bare drywall behind the sink, spreading it with the notched edge of his steel trowel. The repetitive, scraping sound was hypnotically rhythmic. He worked with punishing stamina, his broad shoulders swaying with every precise swiping motion. He pressed the first delicate pink tile into the adhesive, giving it a slight twist to lock it into place.

His scarred, grease-stained hands looked impossibly harsh against the soft pastel ceramic. Yet he handled each piece with obsessive, meticulous care, sliding tiny plastic spacers between the joints to ensure a flawless, uniform gap.

"You are staring," he murmured, not glancing away from the wall.

"I am admiring the craftsmanship."

"You are distracting me." He pressed another tile into the mortar. "Go inventory the vanilla extract."

"The extracts are perfectly aligned. You did that yesterday." I pushed off the table, taking a slow step toward him.

He reached into the box, pulling out another square. The scent of cut pine, wet clay, and his dark coffee hung thick in the air.

I stepped directly behind him. The radiant heat of his solid body enveloped me. I lifted my arms, wrapping them securely around his thick waist. Pressing my chest flush against his wide back, I rested my chin on his shoulder.

Grady went perfectly still. His breathing stalled out in his wide chest. The steel trowel hovered an inch above the wet mortar.

I turned my head slightly, pressing an open-mouthed kiss against the thick cord of muscle at the base of his neck. The taste of salt and honest sweat touched my tongue.

"Keep working," I demanded softly against his skin.

A deep, primal vibration rattled against my ribs as he groaned. "You are playing a very dangerous game right now, Maisie."

"I am just offering moral support." I tightened my grip around his waist, anchoring myself to him.

He resumed spreading the grey adhesive, his movements a fraction slower, deliberately accommodating my presence. The brutal reality of his strength, channeled entirely into building this beautiful, fragile thing for me, stripped away the last ounce of my fear.

We stayed like that for an hour. The harsh overhead lights cast long, domestic shadows across the floorboards. The wall slowly transformed from bare, sterile drywall into a gleaming, perfect expanse of pastel rose.

Grady scraped the excess mortar into the bucket, tossing the dirty trowel into the utility sink. Wiping the wet clay from his knuckles with a shop rag, he turned around within the circle of my arms.

He looked down at me, his dark eyes burning with territorial focus. "The grout needs to cure."

"It looks perfect." I kept my hands linked behind his back.

"It does." He dropped the rag. His large hands settled firmly onto my hips, his long fingers pressing securely into my sides. "But the kitchen is closed for the night. And since you are no longer worried about the budget, you have zero excuses left."

Before I could formulate a reply, he lifted me straight off the floorboards.

The sudden loss of gravity forced a sharp gasp right out of my throat. I grabbed his wide shoulders for balance, my legs instinctively hooking around his thick waist. He carried me with zero effort, his steel-toed boots thudding a relentless rhythm as he marched us out of the kitchen and toward the wooden stairs leading to the apartment.

The fear of falling was completely gone. I buried my face into the curve of his neck, letting the man handle the heavy lifting.

Chapter Fifteen

A Weld That Holds

A Weld That Holds

The wooden spatula scraped against the edge of the stainless steel mixing bowl. I folded the fine almond flour into the stiff, whipped egg whites, counting the strokes under my breath. Fifty-five. Fifty-six. The technique required absolute, unforgiving precision. One fold too few, and the batter sat too thick. One fold too many, and the natural oils separated, turning the expensive mixture into an unusable, runny puddle.

My shoulders ached with a familiar, crushing tension. For my whole life, I carried the weight of the world on my own. Survival meant never leaning on anyone. The moment you did, they either dropped you or handed you the bill.

So why was I letting a massive, broad-shouldered mountain of a contractor systematically dismantle every defense I had?

From across the flour-dusted kitchen, the steady thwack of Grady's hammer echoed in the quiet night. He was rebuilding the collapsed pantry shelves he found me crying over an hour ago. He did not ask questions. He did not offer empty platitudes. He just rolled up his sleeves, measured the heavy oak lumber, and went to work.

The mountain draft seeped through the window frames, fighting a losing battle against the radiant heat of the commercial ovens. I scooped the thick pink batter into a large plastic piping bag, twisting the top tight. My forearms burned. Squeezing uniform, one-inch circles onto the parchment paper forced my muscles into a rigid, painful clench.

I abandoned the piping bag on the prep counter. I turned my head, letting my gaze track the heavy, punishing lines of his body.

The faded denim of his work jeans pulled taut across the staggering width of his thighs. He knelt on the floorboards, angling a heavy power drill against a thick slab of wood. A dark grey thermal shirt clung to his expansive back, defining the heavy, brutal slabs of muscle flexing with every aggressive push of the tool. A single bead of sweat rolled down the thick column of his neck, disappearing into his collar. The heavy leather toolbelt slung low on his hips drew my attention directly to the thick, blunt lines of his waist. His massive, calloused hands gripped the power tool with uncompromising authority.

The man was a machine built for grueling physical endurance. He smelled like cut pine, motor oil, and raw, unfiltered masculine heat. Watching those dirty, scarred hands master the physical world created a reckless, pooling fire right behind my ribs. I wanted those rough palms dragging over my bare thighs. I wanted to map the pale, jagged scars tracking across his forearms with my tongue. The staggering breadth of his shoulders offered a brutal, unyielding shelter. A terrifying, intoxicating desire bloomed in my chest—the desperate urge to just let go. To let him carry it.

The oven timer shrieked.

The sharp electronic noise shattered the quiet. I jumped, my flour-dusted boots slipping on the floorboards. I grabbed a thick protective mitt and yanked the heavy metal oven door open. A blast of three-hundred-degree heat hit my face.

I pulled the wide baking sheet out and set it on the cooling rack.

Disaster.

The delicate almond flour shells were cracked right down the middle. Rough, jagged fissures ruined the smooth tops. The aesthetic was a catastrophic failure. This was batch number five. Five trays of premium, expensive almond flour, imported vanilla bean, and organic egg whites ruined in a single night.

The financial math hit my brain with the force of a stray bullet. Forty dollars of raw materials down the drain. Two hours of meticulous, hand-whisked labor burned to a crisp. The grand opening loomed forty-eight hours away, and my signature pastry was a crumbling, pathetic joke.

The tight, agonizing coil in my lower spine snapped.

My vision blurred. A hot, acidic wave of defeat crawled up my throat. I grabbed the edge of the hot metal tray with my mitt. I did not think. I just reacted to the crushing pressure, the sleepless nights, the terrifying reality of my draining bank account.

I hurled the baking sheet across the room toward the heavy plastic trash bin.

Grady moved.

He abandoned his drill. He lunged across the kitchen space with raw, brutal speed. His heavy work boots scrambled against the wood. He threw his massive frame into the path of the flying metal.

His huge, calloused hand shot out. He caught the blazing hot edge of the baking sheet mid-air.

The aluminum clattered violently against his thick palm. A few cracked macaron shells slid off the parchment paper, shattering onto the floorboards, but the vast majority of the tray remained intact. He lowered the metal sheet slowly, setting it down on a nearby prep table.

He did not flinch from the heat. He did not shout.

He turned his head, fixing me with a dark, uncompromising stare. A muscle feathered in his square jaw.

"What the hell are you doing?" His gravelly voice rumbled low in his chest.

"They are ruined." My hands shook. I pulled the oven mitt off, throwing it onto the counter. "They are dry, cracked, pathetic garbage. Just let them go in the trash, Grady. Let me throw them away."

"They are food."

"They are a failure." I grabbed the edge of the stainless steel table, my knuckles turning white. "Do you know how much that almond flour costs? Do you know the margins I am operating on? I need perfection. I cannot sell cracked shells to a line of paying customers. I am bleeding money, and I cannot even bake a simple French cookie."

Tears burned the corners of my eyes. I refused to let them fall. I tipped my chin up, fighting the overwhelming urge to collapse onto the dirty floorboards.

Grady stared at my rigid posture. He looked at my white-knuckled grip on the metal edge. Then, he looked down at the ruined pastries on the tray.

He reached out. His massive, grease-stained fingers plucked a cracked, deformed pink macaron from the parchment paper.

He lifted the cookie and took a bite.

"Stop." I launched myself forward, grabbing his thick wrist. "Do not eat that. It is dry."

He ignored my desperate grip. He chewed the pastry, his dark eyes never leaving my face. He swallowed. He reached down and picked up another one. He tossed it into his mouth.

"Grady, please." My voice cracked. "They are awful."

"They taste like heaven." He spoke around the crumbling almond flour. "They are sweet. They melt in the mouth."

He ate a third. Then a fourth. He methodically worked his way across the aluminum tray, consuming my ruined efforts with relentless, stubborn determination. He did not care about the aesthetics. He did not care about the jagged lines or the flat bottoms. He devoured the source of my anxiety, piece by piece, turning my catastrophic failure into sustenance.

"Stop eating them," I whispered, the fight draining out of my blood.

"I am hungry." He picked up a fifth cookie. "And you are brilliant. A crack in the shell does not change the flavor, Maisie. You made these with your own hands. They are phenomenal."

"I cannot sell them."

"Then I will eat all of them." He finished the cookie and wiped the pink crumbs from his dark scruff. "Every single batch you mess up, I will finish. You will not waste a single dime of raw material in this kitchen, because I will consume whatever you deem unworthy of the display case."

The psychological armor I wore shattered.

The realization hit my bloodstream, altering the frantic, buzzing panic in my veins. He was not trying to fix the recipe. He was not offering a loan to buy more flour. He was deliberately absorbing the mental blow. By consuming the broken pieces, he validated the labor itself. The crushing pressure in my chest evaporated, replaced by a devastating, hollow ache that demanded release.

My chest hitched. The tears spilled over, tracking hot and fast down my cheeks.

A ragged, ugly sob tore out of my mouth.

Grady abandoned the tray. He crossed the two feet of space between us, his heavy boots thudding against the wood. He wrapped his massive arms around my shoulders and hauled me flush against his rock-solid chest.

I buried my face into the crook of his neck. The scent of cut pine, dark roast coffee, and his warm skin enveloped me. I tangled my fingers into the thick fabric of his thermal shirt, clinging to him like a lifeline in a storm. I cried for the ruined macarons. I cried for the stolen deposit money. I cried for the decade of solitary, grueling survival.

He held me. He absorbed the violent shaking of my petite frame, acting as an unyielding anchor against the flood. His large, rough hand flattened over the back of my head, pressing me deeper into his shelter. His other hand rubbed slow, heavy circles between my shoulder blades, the friction generating a deep, soothing heat.

"I have you." He murmured the raw praise directly against my messy blonde hair. "Let it out. Give it to me, Maisie. I am right here."

"I am so tired." The confession scraped my raw throat.

"I know." He kissed the crown of my head, his dark stubble scratching delightfully against my scalp. "You have been carrying the load alone for a long time. You are done doing that. You belong to me now, and I do not drop what is mine."

The raw, brutal honesty in his gravelly voice broke down the final wall. I surrendered the weight. I let my muscles go slack, allowing his staggering strength to keep me upright. The equalizing power dynamic shifted between us. He was a mountain, but I held the absolute devotion of his heart. He would eat dry cookies, take a hot baking sheet to the bare palm, and stand in the middle of a flour-dusted kitchen at two in the morning just to wipe a tear from my eye.

He respected my ambition, but he refused to let it destroy me.

My sobs slowly tapered off into ragged breaths. The frantic beating of my heart settled into a calm, steady rhythm, matching the heavy thud of his pulse beneath my cheek. I turned my head, resting my ear against his pectoral muscle.

"Your hand." I sniffled, reality returning to the dimly lit kitchen. "You caught a hot pan bare-handed."

"My hands are thick." He kept his arms wrapped securely around my waist. "Takes a lot to burn me."

"Let me see."

I pushed back slightly, breaking the embrace just enough to reach for his right hand. He allowed the movement, turning his broad palm upward under the harsh track lights. A thick, red line marked the calloused skin beneath his thumb, but the flesh was not blistered. Years of swinging hammers and gripping heavy lumber provided a natural layer of dense protection.

I traced the edge of the red mark with my fingertips. The contrast of his rough, scarred skin against my soft touch sent a fresh jolt of heat through my veins.

I lifted his hand. I pressed a soft, open-mouthed kiss directly over the burn.

Grady inhaled sharply. His chest expanded, the muscle pulling taut beneath his shirt.

"I am sorry I threw the tray," I murmured against his palm.

"Throw whatever you need to throw." His voice dropped into a dark, territorial growl. "I will catch it. Every single time."

I lowered his hand, keeping my fingers linked with his. The kitchen was quiet, save for the low hum of the commercial refrigerators. The mess of the failed recipe testing surrounded us—the spilled flour, the cracked shells, the dirty mixing bowls. Tomorrow, the grueling physical labor would begin again. The grand opening still loomed.

But looking up at the harsh, handsome architecture of his face, the terror was gone.

"Come here," he ordered softly.

He did not wait for my compliance. He dropped his grip on my hand, sliding both of his massive arms under my thighs and behind my back. He scooped me straight off the floorboards, lifting my weight with zero effort. My legs instinctively wrapped around his thick waist.

He carried me across the kitchen, maneuvering past the prep tables and the ruined pastries. He carried me out the heavy swinging door, up the creaking wooden stairs, and into the dark, quiet sanctuary of the apartment.

He set me down gently on the edge of the mattress. The old metal springs groaned under the sudden shift.

I watched him unbuckle his heavy leather toolbelt in the shadows. The thick rig hit the floorboards with a heavy thud. He pulled his thermal shirt over his head, the staggering width of his bare chest gleaming in the moonlight filtering through the frosted glass.

Walking to the edge of the bed, he climbed onto the mattress. The wooden frame shrieked in protest. He caged me beneath his massive frame, dropping his heavy weight over my exhausted body. He bracketed my head with his scarred hands, staring down at me with fierce, relentless worship. I reached up, tangling my fingers into his dark hair, and pulled his mouth down to mine.

He kissed me deep, proving once again that the safest place to land was in the rough, calloused hands of a man who built solutions to last.

Chapter Sixteen

Grease-Stained Reverence

The marble slab remained perfectly cold beneath my palms. I pressed the heavy wooden rolling pin into the chilled dough, flattening the thick block of imported butter between the layers of pale flour. Push, roll, fold. The meticulous, repetitive motion of laminating pastry dough usually triggered a dull, throbbing ache in my lower back. Today, my muscles moved with fluid, well-rested ease.

My shoulders were comfortably loose. The frantic, buzzing anxiety that normally governed my mornings was completely absent.

Outside the front window, the low, grating hum of an orbital sander vibrated through the thick glass.

I paused. Wiping my flour-dusted hands on my white canvas apron, I looked through the frosted panes.

Grady knelt on the freshly laid cedar planks of the new front patio. The rhythmic flex of his broad shoulders drew my absolute focus. Sawdust coated the dark grey flannel stretching across his massive back. He looked like a rugged fixture of the mountain itself.

A dangerous, honey-sweet warmth bloomed in my chest. My entire life, I had carried the weight of the world completely alone. Every broken pipe, every looming disaster, every unpaid invoice—it had always rested squarely on my petite shoulders.

Then Grady stepped through my shattered door. This massive man with calloused, scarred hands had not just fixed my collapsing roof; he had systematically dismantled my mental load.

That was the terrifying part. I kept waiting for the catch. People did not just build custom commercial ovens for nothing. They did not gently pry flour-dusted notebooks from my cramped fingers and physically carry me to bed without demanding a toll. If I let myself surrender to his quiet confidence, it would utterly destroy me when he left.

Yet, as Grady wiped his brow with the back of his wrist and looked up through the glass, his gaze holding nothing but pure, unconditional devotion, my frantic heartbeat slowed. I did not just see a contractor anymore. I envisioned Sunday mornings, the scent of warm vanilla, and the intoxicating safety of a shared life.

I abandoned the rolling pin on the marble counter. I grabbed two heavy ceramic mugs from the drying rack and filled them with dark roast coffee. Pressing my hip against the brass handle, I pushed open the heavy front door.

The crisp mountain air bit at my bare arms. The sharp, clean scent of cut western red cedar mixed seamlessly with the exhaust of passing plow trucks.

Grady killed the power to the sander. The sudden silence in the street amplified the heavy thud of his steel-toed boots as he stood up. He dwarfed the space entirely. The crushing weight of his physical presence stole the oxygen straight from my lungs.

He pulled the protective leather gloves off his immense hands, tucking the worn material into his heavy toolbelt. "You should be inside. The wind is freezing."

"I needed a break." I offered him the steaming mug. "And you need caffeine."

He closed the distance between us in two long strides. He did not take the coffee right away. Instead, he reached out, his bare, rough knuckles brushing a stray blonde curl away from my cheek. The blistering friction of his working-man's callouses against my freezing skin sent a heavy jolt of heat straight to my core.

"You are shaking," he murmured. His gravelly voice rumbled low in his expansive chest.

Before I could protest, he set his sander on the railing. He gripped the collar of his thick flannel shirt and pulled it over his head. The staggering width of his chest was displayed in a tight, dark grey thermal. He shook the sawdust off the flannel with a sharp snap of his wrists. He stepped directly into my space, wrapping the heavy, oversized fabric around my petite shoulders.

The radiant heat of his body still clung to the cotton. I immediately pulled the lapels tight under my chin, drowning in the scent of motor oil, dark pine, and his unfiltered masculine heat.

"Better?" he asked, his dark eyes tracking my face with territorial focus.

"Much better." I handed him the mug.

He took it, his massive fingers completely dwarfing the thick ceramic handle. He drank the scalding black coffee in three long swallows, completely ignoring the burning temperature. He lowered the mug, resting his hip back against the sturdy cedar railing he had just built.

"The wood looks beautiful, Grady." I traced my hand over the flawlessly sanded edge of the perimeter fence. The joints were completely seamless, the countersunk screws hidden with meticulous, obsessive care.

"It will hold up to the winter snow." He set the empty mug down on a nearby sawhorse. "I am sealing it this afternoon. But I left a six-inch gap along the top runner." He pointed a thick, scarred finger toward the edge facing the street. "For the window boxes. What kind of flowers do you want in them?"

My throat tightened. I pulled the flannel closer around my ribs. "I crossed exterior decorations off the list last night. The wholesale butter delivery for the opening week ate the remaining surplus. We cannot afford custom planters."

Grady stepped fully into my space. He planted his heavy work boots squarely on the cedar planks, completely blocking the freezing wind blowing off the street. He reached out, resting his large, warm hands on my shoulders.

"I am not asking for your budget, Maisie. I am asking for your favorite color."

"Grady, the lumber alone—"

"I built the boxes at my workshop last night out of scrap cedar." He cut me off, his voice a steady, unyielding anchor. "I loaded the potting soil into the bed of my truck this morning. Everything is already handled. I just need to know what to plant in the dirt. You do the baking. Let me handle the heavy lifting."

The defensive armor I kept strapped to my ribs fractured. He did not wait for my permission to solve my problems. He anticipated the obstacles and destroyed them before they ever reached my desk.

"Yellow." My voice cracked perfectly down the middle. "I love yellow daffodils."

A dark amusement lit his harsh features. "Then I will plant yellow daffodils."

He dropped his hands from my shoulders, turning his attention to the large industrial drop cloth spread across the threshold of the bakery door. He bent down, carefully folding the thick canvas inward to trap the loose wood shavings. He hauled the heavy fabric over his shoulder, ensuring not a single speck of dust breached the pristine interior of my commercial kitchen.

"You do not have to clean that up right now," I protested softly.

"I am not tracking debris onto your clean floorboards." He tossed the folded canvas into the bed of his truck. "You spent two hours sweeping this morning. Your workspace stays perfect."

He unbuckled his heavy leather toolbelt. The thick rig hit the bed of the truck with a loud, metallic clatter. Stripped of his tools, the raw, massive architecture of his body was completely undeniable. Thick cords of muscle stood out on his arms. The faded denim of his work jeans pulled taut across the staggering width of his thighs.

He walked back onto the patio. He stopped in front of the wide, built-in wooden bench he had constructed near the front window. He brushed a few stray wood shavings off the smooth surface with his thick palm. Then, he sat down, bracing his heavy boots wide on the planks.

He looked up at me. His square jaw set in stone.

"Come here," he ordered gently.

I did not hesitate. The agonizing terror of failing alone, the constant, suffocating need to remain independent at all costs, completely evaporated in the afternoon sun. I stepped right between his parted knees.

He wrapped his massive, grease-stained arms around my waist. He pulled me forward, lifting me entirely off the heavy cedar planks.

I landed hard against his thick denim, the solid, unyielding heat of his body anchoring me completely to the earth.

I wrapped my arms around his wide neck, burying my face into the crook of his shoulder. He rested his chin on the top of my blonde head. His enormous hands smoothed down my spine, mapping the curve of my back through the oversized flannel. He held me with the exact same meticulous, obsessive care he used to build the foundational walls of the shop.

"You work too hard," he praised, his gravelly voice vibrating directly against my chest. "You are doing phenomenal, Maisie. Everything is ready. Just rest for a minute."

"I can rest when the doors open," I whispered, though I made absolutely no move to climb off his lap.

"You can rest right now." He pressed a warm, open-mouthed kiss to the pulse jumping at my throat. "I have you. I am never dropping you."

The mountain town continued to move entirely around us. A passing plow truck rumbled down the icy street. Locals bundled in heavy winter coats walked the opposing sidewalks. Yet, seated on the sturdy cedar bench, wrapped securely in the rough, calloused hands of a man who built solutions to last, the chaotic world outside ceased to exist. The foundation was perfectly secure.

Chapter Seventeen

A Crack in the Foundation

The rhythmic, grating hum of the orbital sander vibrated through the floorboards. I folded the heavy cinnamon dough over the cold marble slab, pushing the heels of my hands deep into the pale flour. I pressed, rolled, and turned the mass, establishing a steady, predictable pace.

Grady knelt beside the custom-welded pastry display racks he had built from scratch. He dragged a block of heavy grit sandpaper along the steel joints, ensuring the metal was entirely smooth. He wore a faded, dark grey thermal shirt pushed up past his elbows. Thick cords of muscle flexed in his forearms with every aggressive, sweeping motion. Sawdust and fine metal shavings coated his heavy denim jeans.

The scent of cut pine mingled heavily with the warm yeast of the cinnamon rolls rising on the nearby prep table.

For the first time in my fiercely independent life, I was not drowning in stress. I watched the steady, punishing stamina of his broad shoulders. I desperately wanted to surrender. I wanted to sink completely into the quiet, unshakeable sanctuary he built with those calloused hands. Every time he silently took a broken piece of my bakery, or my exhausting mental load, and entirely repaired it, a terrifying, delicious warmth spread through my petite frame.

It was entirely too easy to let him carry my weight. And that was exactly what terrified me.

I had spent my entire life learning the hard way that the only person I could count on was myself. When my old apartment flooded, I bailed the water with a plastic bucket.

When the former contractor robbed me of my deposit and left this building in ruins, I had not called for help. I had bought a cheap hammer and started swinging. Ambition was my solitary armor. If I finally leaned on Grady—if I actually trusted this golden, unconditional worship was permanent—what would happen when reality finally struck? The universe did not just hand out miracles without exacting a brutal price.

I was waiting for the other shoe to drop. My muscles coiled tight despite the comforting, steady hum of his sander. Nothing this perfect was allowed to last.

Outside the frosted front windows, the afternoon sky shifted. The pale, winter sunlight vanished beneath a thick, rolling blanket of iron-grey clouds. The temperature inside the bakery dropped ten degrees in a matter of minutes. The sudden chill bit through my thin canvas apron.

Grady killed the power to the sander. The sudden silence hung heavy in the room. He stood up from the floorboards, wiping a streak of dark grease from his jaw with the back of his massive wrist. He turned his attention to the windows. The sheer size of his frame blocked the remaining natural light.

"Wind is picking up." His gravelly voice rumbled low in his expansive chest.

"The forecast said we might get a few inches tonight." I laid a damp cotton towel over the rising dough.

"That is not a few inches." He walked to the front door and pushed the heavy wood open. A vicious, howling gust of freezing air immediately bit into the warm room. Snowflakes the size of quarters swirled violently through the gap, landing on his heavy work boots. "The temperature just bottomed out. That is a late-season system dropping right over the ridge. Town is going to be buried by nightfall."

He pushed the door shut, throwing the heavy brass deadbolt into place with a loud crack. He immediately shifted his focus back to the kitchen, his dark eyes scanning the room for any unsealed drafts. He did not panic. He simply assessed the structural integrity of the box he had built around me.

"I need to check the roof flashing over the pantry," he decided, grabbing his heavy leather toolbelt from the nearby counter. "I will bring in more firewood for the stove upstairs when I am done. Do not go out back. The ice on the alley stairs is already freezing solid."

"I will stay right here," I promised.

He buckled the heavy leather rig around his thick waist. He walked past me, stopping just long enough to press a hard, open-mouthed kiss to the top of my head. The raw, completely unfiltered devotion in that simple gesture made my chest ache. Then, he pushed through the swinging back door, disappearing into the utility corridor.

Left alone in the quiet kitchen, I moved to the stainless steel sink to wash my hands. The hot water cascaded over my knuckles. I scrubbed the sticky dough from my skin, my mind racing through the prep list.

The grand opening was exactly three days away. Friday morning at six o'clock. The display cases were bolted to the floorboards. The plumbing was pristine. The custom ovens were fully calibrated. All that remained was the actual food production.

My phone vibrated violently against the metal prep counter.

A sharp, persistent electronic chime echoed in the empty room. I shut off the faucet. I grabbed a dry towel, wiping my hands as I walked over to the device. The screen illuminated with a high-priority push notification from the commercial freight company.

I discarded the towel. I tapped the screen. The email expanded.

FREIGHT ALERT: Route 40 Mountain Pass Closed.

DUE TO SEVERE LATE-SEASON BLIZZARD CONDITIONS, ALL COMMERCIAL TRANSIT OVER THE RIDGE HAS BEEN SUSPENDED. YOUR DELIVERY (PALLET 4402 - INDUSTRIAL PLANETARY MIXERS) HAS BEEN TURNED AROUND AT THE COUNTY WEIGH STATION. ESTIMATED DELAY: 72 TO 96 HOURS.

The blood drained entirely from my face. I read the abrasive black text three times, desperately hoping the words would miraculously rearrange themselves. They did not change. The pass was closed. The machinery was gone.

I slowly lifted my head. I stared at the cold, bare expanse of the reinforced steel table situated against the far wall. I had left that eight-foot section completely empty. It was the designated home for my two custom-ordered, thirty-quart planetary mixers.

Three hundred pounds of prep work without industrial mixers meant doing it all by hand.

The brutal, mathematical reality of the situation hit my brain like a physical blow. Fifty pounds of French buttercream. Eighty pounds of brioche dough. Forty pounds of delicate macaron batter. Mixing that sheer volume of heavy, resistant ingredients by hand was biologically impossible for a single person. My arms would completely give out before the first sunrise. The butter would separate. The dough would dry out. The entire opening day inventory would be completely ruined.

I had zero backup plan. The upgraded plumbing and the premium pastel tiles had drained the emergency fund entirely. I could not buy replacement equipment locally, even if the town hardware store carried commercial-grade machinery, which they did not.

My hands began to shake. A cold sweat broke across the back of my neck.

The frantic, buzzing anxiety I thought Grady had cured roared back to life, flooding my veins with acidic terror. This was the exact catastrophe I had been waiting for. The universe was finally demanding its toll. The shop was beautiful, the foundation was flawless, but without the means to produce the product, I was entirely bankrupt.

I dropped the phone onto the steel table. The metal clattered loudly.

Survival instinct kicked in, overriding logic. I turned toward the utility drawer. I yanked the heavy metal handle open. The metal tracks screeched in protest. I grabbed the largest manual wire whisk I owned. I dragged a massive, thirty-quart stainless steel mixing bowl off the bottom shelf and slammed it onto the prep counter.

I had to start now. If I whisked the buttercream by hand, it would take five times as long. I would not sleep for the next seventy-two hours. I marched toward the walk-in refrigerator, my chest hitching with panicked, jagged breaths. I hauled out three ten-pound blocks of wholesale butter. I dropped them onto the counter with a heavy thud.

I grabbed a chef's knife and began hacking the cold, solid blocks into smaller cubes. My hands trembled so violently against the handle that the blade slipped, nearly catching my index finger.

I ignored the near-miss. I shoved the cold butter cubes into the massive metal bowl. I dumped a heavy bag of powdered sugar over the top. The white dust plumed violently into the air. I grabbed the wire whisk. I gripped the handle with both hands and drove it down into the cold, dense butter.

It did not budge. The mixture was practically concrete.

I threw my entire body weight over the bowl, forcing the wire loops through the fat and sugar. My shoulders burned immediately. The friction tore at my palms. I dragged the whisk through the mixture again. And again. And again. A desperate, ragged sound tore out of my throat. I was not making a dent. I was scraping the surface of a mountain with a toothpick.

"Maisie."

The gravelly, commanding voice cut through my frantic spiral.

I did not stop. I could not stop. If I stopped moving, the crushing reality of the failure would pull me completely under. I dragged the whisk through the dense butter, tears of absolute frustration blurring my vision.

"I have to mix it." I shoved the wire loops into the sugar. "I have to get it soft."

Heavy boots thudded rapidly across the wood floor.

Grady did not ask for permission. He stepped directly behind me. His massive, calloused hands clamped over my wrists. His grip was absolute iron, entirely overpowering my frantic movements without causing an ounce of pain. He physically halted the whisk.

"Let go of the metal." He rumbled the order next to my ear.

"I cannot!" My voice cracked perfectly down the middle. "The mixers are not coming. The pass is shut down, Grady. The truck got turned around at the weigh station. I have three hundred pounds of batter to make, and I have to do it by hand. I have to start right now."

"Let go of the whisk."

"Please, I need to—"

He smoothly pried my rigid fingers off the handle. He tossed the whisk onto the counter. It hit the stainless steel with a loud clatter, rolling away into the spilled sugar.

He caught my hips and physically spun me around.

I slammed flush against his solid, broad chest. The staggering width of his body blocked out the entire kitchen. He was a mountain of thermal cotton, raw muscle, and protective heat. He looked down at me. A muscle feathered in his square jaw.

"Look at me." He gripped my upper arms, anchoring my shaking frame.

I tipped my chin up. The tears finally spilled over, tracking hot and fast down my cheeks.

"I am going to fail." The confession scraped my throat. "Three days before the opening, and I am completely dead in the water. I have no product to sell. I spent every dime I had on this building."

"You are not failing." He lifted his hands, framing my face with his rough, grease-stained palms. His thick thumbs swept the tears off my skin with terrifying gentleness. "Take a breath. The building is secure. The power is on. You are safe."

"I do not have the equipment." The panic clawed at my throat, making it impossible to drag an adequate amount of air into my lungs. "The math does not work. One person cannot manually produce the required volume. It is biologically impossible."

"Then it is a good thing you are not one person anymore."

The absolute, raw certainty in his gravelly voice acted as a direct counter-weight to my terror. The frantic beating of my heart stuttered against my ribs.

He dropped his hands from my face. He turned slightly, his dark eyes scanning the massive steel bowl filled with cold butter. He looked at the white sugar coating my apron. He looked at the discarded phone sitting on the far table. He processed the logistical failure in a matter of seconds. He did not offer empty platitudes. He did not tell me it was going to be okay. He immediately formulated a structural solution.

"The main roads out of town are buried." I desperately tried to maintain my grip on reality. "The plows will not clear the pass until Sunday. The freight company operates strictly on commercial routes. They will not risk their trucks on the ice."

"I do not care about the commercial freight company." Grady turned back to me. His chest expanded as he drew in a deep breath. "I care about your bakery."

He reached down, gripping my waist. He hoisted me straight off the floorboards, lifting me easily onto the clear edge of the prep counter. The cold steel seeped through my jeans, but his massive body stood directly between my parted knees, blocking the chill. He crowded deep into my space, resting his large hands securely on my thighs. The blistering friction of his heavy callouses grounded my racing mind.

"Listen to me very carefully," he ordered, holding my absolute focus. "You are not hand-whipping three hundred pounds of batter. I will not allow you to break your body to piece this together. You will ruin your wrists, and I am not letting that happen."

"Then what do I do?" The fight drained out of my blood, leaving a hollow, devastating ache behind. "I have lines of locals expecting a grand opening on Friday. I promised them food."

"You are going to walk upstairs." He smoothed his thumbs over the denim covering my legs. "You are going to take a hot shower. You are going to put on the thickest, warmest sweater you own, and you are going to sit by the woodstove."

"Grady, I have to fix this."

"I am fixing this." His grip tightened slightly on my thighs, a firm, possessive pressure that demanded total compliance. "You bake the bread, Maisie. I handle the heavy lifting. That was the deal."

"You cannot control the weather."

"No. But I know every single contractor, bar owner, and restaurant supplier within a fifty-mile radius." A dark, territorial resolve hardened his harsh features. "I poured the concrete foundations for half the commercial kitchens in this county. I know exactly who has industrial mixers, and I know exactly who owes me a favor."

My lungs seized. I stared at the rugged architecture of his face, the pale scars tracking across his jawline. He was entirely serious. He was going to leverage a decade of his own backbreaking labor just to acquire temporary equipment for my shop.

"The roads are closed," I reminded him weakly.

"The highway is closed to commercial transit." He corrected smoothly. "My buddy drives a heavy-duty county plow truck. I can get through the back access roads if I follow his salt spreaders. If there is a thirty-quart planetary mixer sitting idle in this mountain range, I will find it. I will unbolt it from the floor myself, and I will haul it through the blizzard."

The protective armor I wore for ten years systematically dissolved under the crushing weight of his devotion. I did not want to argue logistics anymore. I did not want to be the sole architect of my own survival. I raised my hands, sliding my fingers deep into his dark hair, and pulled his face toward mine.

He caught my mouth in a fierce, consuming kiss.

He stripped away the lingering panic, driving his dominant heat directly into my system. He tasted like dark coffee and utter, unyielding safety. I opened for him willingly, dragging my tongue against his. I wrapped my arms around his wide neck, anchoring myself to the solid mountain of his body.

He stepped completely into the space between my legs, his hips pressing flush against the counter. He wrapped his massive arms entirely around my waist, lifting me a few inches off the steel just to hold my weight against his chest. I hooked my ankles behind his thick thighs. The physical contrast of his staggering size against my petite frame obliterated any remaining trace of my fear.

Outside the frosted glass, the wind shrieked against the newly reinforced cedar patio. The storm threatened to bury the entire town in white. But inside the warm kitchen, surrounded by the scent of pine and his raw masculine heat, the threat completely neutralized.

He slowly pulled back. He rested his forehead against mine. His breathing was heavy, the air rattling deep in his wide chest.

"I have you," he promised roughly. "I am going to make some calls. You are going upstairs."

I nodded once. I let my hands fall to his broad shoulders. "Okay."

He set me back down on the floorboards. He did not ask for a single thing in return. He turned around, picked up his phone from the cold steel table, and walked toward the back office to go to work. Outside, the blizzard howled against the frosted glass.

Chapter Eighteen

The Mechanics of Praise

I could frame a house from the foundation up blindfolded, but standing this close to Maisie makes my scarred hands tremble. She is so damn small. A fierce, flour-dusted hurricane of blonde hair and stubborn pride, used to carrying the entire world on shoulders that barely reach my sternum. I want to take it all from her. Every broken pipe, every canceled delivery, every ounce of her exhaustion.

My desire for her is a living, breathing obsession hammering against my ribs. I want to worship the linoleum floor she bakes on. But that is exactly what terrifies me. If I touch her the way I am dying to—if I let her see the consuming magnitude of my need to wrap my frame around hers and shield her from the universe—I might spook her. She spent her whole life fighting alone.

Upstairs in the apartment, the blizzard shrieks against the glass. The woodstove pops, throwing orange light across the small room. Maisie paces the floorboards. Her hands shake as she runs her fingers through her messy hair. The adrenaline of the ruined freight delivery still hums in her veins.

"I have to go back down." She turns toward the door. "If I start whisking the buttercream now, I can get exactly one batch done before midnight."

I block the exit. I do not crowd her, but I leave absolutely no room for escape. "You are not touching a whisk tonight."

Her chin tips up. The fight in her expression is beautiful, but it is tearing her apart. I step forward, catching her hips. The tension radiating off her petite frame is a physical static. I guide her backward until the backs of her knees hit the edge of the mattress. She drops onto the quilt.

Kneeling on the hardware-store rug between her parted legs, I reach for her shoulders. My thumbs dig into the tight, knotted muscles at the base of her neck. She gasps, her spine going rigid, before collapsing forward into the pressure.

"Let it go," I order quietly, working the punishing knot out of her collarbone. "You are safe up here. The shop is locked. The storm cannot touch you."

I drag my knuckles down the curve of her spine, pressing the lingering panic straight out of her system. The frantic, jagged rhythm of her breathing slows against my chest as I knead the sore spots between her shoulder blades. She melts into my hands. The frantic baker terrified of a failed opening vanishes, replaced by a devastatingly soft woman seeking shelter.

She lifts her head. Her gaze drags up my body, stripping away my defenses with terrifying precision. Her eyes track the grease permanently stained into my knuckles, tracing the pale, jagged scars crossing my forearms. She looks at the tight, dark thermal stretched across my chest, her pupils dilating as she inhales the scent of cut pine and sawdust clinging to my clothes. The raw, unfiltered hunger in her expression halts the oxygen in my throat. She is not just looking at a contractor. She is looking at a machine built for endurance, and she wants me to use every ounce of that stamina on her.

"Take it off," she demands softly.

My heart stutters. I grip the hem of my shirt and pull it over my head, tossing the cotton onto the floorboards. The firelight catches the shadows of my ribs and the corded muscle of my abdomen.

Maisie reaches out. Her soft, flour-dusted fingers graze the center of my chest, tracing the line of dark hair trailing down to the waistband of my denim. The blistering contrast of her delicate touch against my rough exterior sends a reckless heat straight to my core. She grips the leather of my belt and pulls me closer.

The equalizing shift between us hits me like a freight train. She is tiny, a fragile bird I could crush by accident, but right now, she holds every ounce of my emotional power. I am entirely at her mercy.

"Make me forget about the bakery," she whispers, her thumbs hooking under the metal buckle. "Burn it out of my head, Grady."

I do not need to be told twice. I stand up, shedding my boots and denim in a matter of seconds. When I drop back onto the mattress, the old springs shriek in protest. I crowd her backward into the pillows, caging her beneath me.

My calloused hands grip the hem of her sweater, pulling the thick wool over her head. Her jeans follow, leaving her completely bare in the firelight. Her soft, pale skin against the dark quilt destroys the last thread of my restraint.

I bracket her head with my arms, lowering my mouth to the crook of her neck. The taste of salt, vanilla, and pure, unfiltered woman touches my tongue. She arches up, her fingernails biting half-moons into the skin of my back.

"I am right here," I rumble against her collarbone, pressing a hard, open-mouthed kiss over her pulse. "Give me the weight, Maisie. Let me carry it."

"Grady." The plea tears out of her throat.

I slide down her body, my rough thumbs tracking over the soft expanse of her thighs. I part her knees, settling myself directly over her center. The heat radiating from her is intoxicating. I bury my face between her legs, dragging my tongue deep.

She violently shudders. Her hands tangle into my dark hair, holding me down as if she fears I might walk away. I have absolutely no intention of stopping. I work her with single-minded, territorial focus, using the exact same meticulous obsession I apply to building load-bearing walls. I map every nerve, every flinch, demanding her total surrender.

"You taste like heaven," I praise roughly, scraping my teeth gently against her sensitive flesh.

"Please," she begs, her hips bucking off the mattress. "Now. I need you now."

I crawl back up her body, settling my hips right between her thighs. She is so thoroughly wrecked, so slick and ready for me, that the mere sight of her ruins my solitary existence. I catch both of her wrists, pinning them securely to the pillows above her head. She does not fight the restraint; she leans into the absolute control.

I align myself with her core and push forward.

The size difference forces a sharp, fractured gasp right out of her mouth as I slide inside. I fill her completely, stretching her tight. I freeze, gritting my teeth against the blinding sensation of her velvet heat wrapping around me. The friction is pure agony.

"Am I hurting you?" The question grates out of my chest.

"No." She arches her spine, forcing me an inch deeper. "Do not stop. Please, Grady."

I drop my iron grip on control. I draw back and drive into her again, setting a relentless, punishing rhythm. The wooden bedframe slams against the drywall. I anchor her pinned wrists with one hand, using my free arm to slide under her lower back, lifting her hips to take the full length of my drive.

"You take me so well," I drop the praise directly against her ear, my breathing ragged. "So damn perfectly."

Her nails dig into my palm where our fingers are laced together. The frantic panic that owned her downstairs is entirely gone, replaced by a desperate, consuming fire. We meet each other blow for blow. She is fiercely ambitious, refusing to just lie back and take it. She meets my thrusts, her hips snapping up to demand more depth, more friction, more of me.

"I need you," she cries out, the words fracturing as I grind against her center. "I cannot do this without you."

The confession shatters the concrete armor around my heart. "You never have to. I am never leaving this room. I am never leaving you."

I increase the pace, driving us toward the edge with uncompromising efficiency. Sweat beads on my shoulders, dripping onto her flushed chest. The friction builds into a blinding crescendo. Her control snaps. The delicate muscles of her core clench violently around me.

She shatters, calling out my name in a high, breathless sob. The force of her climax drags me entirely over the cliff right alongside her. I bury myself to the hilt, groaning as the release rips through my bloodstream. The world outside the frosted glass drops away completely.

For a long time, the only sound in the apartment is the harsh scrape of our breathing and the crackle of the woodstove. I collapse to the side, taking my weight off her petite frame, but I refuse to let her go. I haul her flush against my chest, wrapping my arms around her waist to anchor her to the mattress.

Her head rests perfectly over my heart. The erratic drumming of my pulse slows as her fingertips lazily trace the scars on my pectoral muscle. The storm outside continues to rage, dumping white powder over the mountain town. The roads are closed. The commercial delivery truck is miles away.

But looking down at her softly parted lips and relaxed shoulders, the logistical failure means absolutely nothing. She is entirely safe. The panic is gone, burned out by the physical connection forging us together.

"The batter," she murmurs sleepily against my collarbone.

"Is chilling in the walk-in." I pull the thick quilt up over her bare shoulders, tucking the fabric securely under her chin. "I will handle the equipment, Maisie. You rest."

She does not argue. The fight is completely drained from her system. She closes her eyes, succumbing to the exhaustion she has been holding at bay for ten years.

I wait until her breathing evens out into a deep, restorative rhythm. Carefully, meticulously, I slide out from beneath the covers. The cold air of the room bites at my bare skin, but I ignore it. I step into my discarded jeans, fastening the metal button.

I pick up my phone from the nightstand. The screen illuminates, casting a harsh blue glow over my calloused hands. I pull up the contact list I have built over a decade of pouring concrete and framing roofs. If there is a loaner mixer buried somewhere in this county, I am going to find it.

I cross the quiet room. A scrap of drywall paper sits on the scarred wood of the kitchen table. I uncap a black pen and go to work.

Chapter Nineteen

Mapping the Rebuild

I stared at the water-stained ceiling, my pen hovering over a battered legal pad. *Action Plan.* I underlined the words twice, the ink bleeding into the cheap paper. Step one: fix the plumbing. Step two: rebuild the display cases. Step three: stop relying on Grady.

The third step was the hardest. My entire life, I had carried the weight of the world on my own shoulders. Help always came with a hidden price tag, a debt I would eventually have to repay. But then Grady had ducked his massive frame through my shattered front door, his heavy toolbelt clinking, and completely upended my survival instincts.

God, I wanted to let him. The desire was a heavy, sweet ache in my chest. I wanted to surrender this exhausting uphill battle, to just melt into his broad shoulders and let his scarred, calloused hands fix everything. When he looked at me, there were no games, no expectations—just a quiet, steady devotion that terrified me. If I let down my guard, if I actually let him take on my mental load, what would happen when he realized I was just as broken as this bakery?

I gripped the pen tighter. I needed a plan.

The mountain wind shrieked against the frosted glass of the bedroom window. The blizzard outside was systematically burying the town in white, erasing the roads, and cutting off my only hope of a commercial freight delivery. The thirty-quart planetary mixers were sitting in a weigh station fifty miles away. Without them, three hundred pounds of delicate French buttercream and heavy brioche dough required grueling manual labor. My wrists throbbed just thinking about the friction. I had to start right now. I had to go downstairs into the freezing kitchen, grab a wire whisk, and fight the dense butter until my joints gave out.

I threw the heavy quilt off my bare legs. The icy air of the apartment bit at my skin. I pulled on a pair of soft thermal leggings and an oversized gray sweater, determined to maintain absolute control over my own failure. I refused to let an avalanche of circumstances drown me while I slept. I moved out of the bedroom, my bare feet silent on the cold wood floorboards.

A low circle of yellow light illuminated the small kitchen table. I stopped walking.

Grady sat in the heavy oak chair. He wore his faded denim jeans, his chest completely bare. The staggering width of his back blocked the light from the woodstove. He held his phone to his ear, a heavy black pen gripped in his right hand. A ragged scrap of drywall paper covered the table, entirely marked up with dark ink, rough measurements, and phone numbers. Beside the paper, an old, rugged tablet displayed a glowing green-and-red weather radar map.

"Yeah, Mike. I see the radar." His gravelly voice rumbled low, vibrating against the quiet walls. "The storm cell is stalling over the ridge. How far out is your salt spreader?"

A pause. Grady dragged a rough hand through his dark hair, a muscle feathering in his square jaw.

"Forty minutes? Good. Keep your blade dropped low. I am taking my rig out, and I am drafting right behind you down the access road. Yes, I have chains on the tires. Do not slow down for me, just clear the ice."

He ended the call. He stabbed the pen onto the drywall scrap, crossing out a name. He immediately dialed another number, pressing the phone back to his ear. He did not look exhausted. He looked like a machine calculating structural loads, completely immune to the panic tearing my stomach apart.

"Frank." Grady leaned forward, bracing his thick forearms on the wood. "I know the pass is buried. I do not care about the highway. I need a thirty-quart planetary mixer. Tonight."

The person on the other end protested. The tinny sound of a frantic voice leaked from the phone speaker. Grady did not flinch.

"I poured the concrete foundation for your diner for cost, Frank. I am calling in the marker. You have that backup Hobart unit sitting in storage. I am coming to get it." He paused, listening to the man yield. "Make sure the bowl and the paddle attachments are with it. I will be at your loading dock in an hour."

My lungs burned for air. I braced my hand against the doorframe, my knuckles turning perfectly white. He was doing it. He was sitting at my cheap kitchen table at three in the morning, systematically leveraging a decade of his own backbreaking labor just to save my grand opening. He was not asking for a percentage of the profits. He was not asking for his name on the lease. He was preparing to drive a heavy truck through a blinding blizzard for me because he simply refused to let me fail.

The defensive armor I had spent ten years building violently shattered. The staggering anxiety over the missing freight truck evaporated, replaced by an absolute, desperate need. I did not want to survive alone anymore. I wanted to build a life inside the concrete safety of his shadow.

I closed the distance between us.

Grady ended the call, tossing the phone onto the table. He leaned forward, staring at the logistical map he had drawn on the drywall paper. I stepped right between his parted knees.

He looked up. His dark eyes instantly tracked my face. "You are supposed to be sleeping," he commanded softly, reaching out to rest his massive hands on my hips.

"You cannot drive in this storm." My voice shook, betraying the raw terror blooming in my chest. "The roads are sheets of solid ice. The plow trucks are barely making it through. If you slide off the ridge—"

"I am not sliding off the ridge." His large thumbs smoothed over the soft cotton of my sweater, pressing a grounding, heavy heat into my waist. "My truck is weighed down with four hundred pounds of sand in the bed, and I have heavy chains on the tires. I know every curve of this mountain blindfolded."

"It is a baking mixer, Grady." I grabbed his thick wrists, my fingers entirely dwarfed by the staggering size of his forearms. "It is not worth your life. We can delay the opening. I can post a sign. I can—"

"You are not delaying anything." The absolute certainty in his gravelly voice acted as a physical anchor. He squeezed my hips, demanding my total compliance. "You spent every dime you had on the pastel tiles and the custom plumbing. You fought the local zoning board for a month. You stayed awake for three days straight testing almond flour ratios. I will not let a late-season snowstorm steal this from you. I handle the heavy lifting. That was the deal."

"I cannot let you pay my debts."

"You do not have any debts." He shifted closer, pulling me flush against the solid wall of his bare chest. "You belong to me. Your bakery is my bakery. Your problems are my problems. I am going to follow the county plow down the access road, I am going to load that Hobart mixer into my truck, and I am going to bolt it to your floorboards before the sun comes up."

The fight drained entirely out of my bloodstream. He was not giving me an option. He was systematically removing every obstacle in my path with brutal, terrifying efficiency. The magnitude of his devotion stripped away my pride, leaving a hollow, devastating ache that demanded an immediate connection.

I did not answer him with words. I pushed the heavy legal pad and the scrap of drywall paper completely off the table. They hit the floorboards with a soft thud. I dragged my hands into his dark hair, gripping the thick strands, and pulled his mouth directly to mine.

The kiss was not sweet or gentle. It was a frantic, punishing collision of teeth and desperate heat. I drove my tongue past his lips, demanding everything he had to give. The raw, unfiltered intensity of my surrender hit him like a physical blow. He groaned, a deep, territorial sound that rumbled straight from his expansive chest into mine.

His massive hands clamped onto my thighs. He stood up, lifting my weight entirely off the floorboards, and threw me back against the heavy steel of the apartment refrigerator. The cold metal bit sharply through my sweater, a shocking contrast to the blazing furnace of his body pressing flush against my front.

"Maisie." He tore his mouth away, his breathing ragged. The air rattled deep in his wide chest. He anchored my waist, his thumbs digging into the thermal fabric of my leggings. "What is wrong? Tell me."

"Give it to me." My voice fractured, completely devoid of independence. "I need you. Right now."

He did not ask another question. The equalizing power dynamic tipped perfectly into place. He recognized the desperate, consuming fire in my system, and he met it with devastating force. He gripped the hem of my sweater, shoving the thick wool up to my collarbone. His calloused, scarred hands dragged down my bare ribs, the blistering friction of his working-man's skin burning a trail of absolute ownership into my flesh. He yanked my thermal leggings down, his rough knuckles grazing the sensitive skin of my thighs.

I hooked my legs firmly around his thick waist, abandoning my footing and my carefully constructed boundaries entirely. He unbuttoned his denim, freeing himself in the shadows. The staggering mass of his body caged me against the appliance. He aligned his hips with mine, the blunt, heavy heat of him pressing directly against my entrance.

"Look at me," he commanded, his gravelly voice dropping an octave.

I tipped my chin down. I fixed my gaze on his harsh, handsome face. The pale scars tracking his jawline stood out in the dim, yellow light of the kitchen.

He drove forward. He sank deep into my wet heat in one brutal, uncompromising thrust. The stretch ripped a high, sharp gasp right out of my throat. I arched my spine against the refrigerator door, taking the absolute fullness of him. He anchored my hips with his iron grip, establishing a relentless, driving rhythm. The appliance rattled violently against the drywall.

"You are mine," he rasped, his teeth scraping over my collarbone. "I am fixing this. I am fixing everything."

"I know." I dug my nails into the thick muscle of his wide shoulders, anchoring myself to the only solid refuge in the room. "I trust you."

The confession fueled him. He increased the pace, his hips snapping forward with punishing stamina. The friction was a blazing inferno. I rode the heavy, desperate impacts, entirely surrendering my control to the massive builder holding me completely off the ground. He possessed me with the exact same single-minded, obsessive focus he used to assemble structural beams.

"You take me perfectly," he praised in a dark, gravelly whisper, grinding his hips deep to hit the most sensitive bundle of nerves. "Give it all to me. Let it go."

The tension coiled tight in my lower stomach, rising exponentially with every single thrust. The terror of the failing business, the exhausting physical labor of the past month, and the terrifying prospect of him driving into the blizzard all compressed into a blinding, white-hot point of pressure.

My vision blurred entirely. The small apartment kitchen vanished, narrowing down to the scent of cut pine, motor oil, and the intoxicating reality of his unyielding strength. I shattered around him, calling out his name in a ragged sob. The violent contractions milked him deep. A second later, he groaned, burying his face into the crook of my neck as his own blinding climax tore through his massive frame.

We stayed pinned against the refrigerator for a long time. The erratic hammering of his pulse eventually slowed against my chest.

I kept my face buried in the curve of his neck, breathing in the scent of sawdust and warm skin. His large hands rested securely on my lower back, keeping me elevated off the floorboards without a single ounce of fatigue. The storm outside continued to howl against the windowpanes, but the frantic, buzzing terror that had owned my mind for the past ten hours was completely gone. The foundation was secure.

He withdrew slowly, the loss of his physical presence drawing a soft protest from my lips. He ignored my complaint, stepping back just enough to retrieve my clothing. With meticulous, protective care, he pulled my thermal leggings back up to my waist. He smoothed the oversized gray sweater down over my ribs, ensuring I was completely shielded from the cold air of the kitchen. He adjusted his own denim, fastening the metal button with swift efficiency.

He scooped me entirely into his arms, carrying me away from the cold kitchen and back into the dark warmth of the bedroom. The old mattress sank under his overwhelming weight. He laid me in the exact center of the bed, pulling the thick quilt up securely under my chin. He reached down, his scarred knuckles brushing a damp curl away from my forehead.

"I am leaving in ten minutes," he promised softly, his dark eyes burning with territorial focus. "I will follow the county plow all the way to the diner. When you wake up, that commercial mixer will be sitting in your bakery."

"Be careful," I whispered, my eyelids growing heavy.

"Always." He leaned down, pressing a hard kiss to my mouth. "Sleep, Maisie. I handle the heavy lifting."

He turned and walked out of the bedroom. The heavy thud of his steel-toed boots echoed through the apartment, followed by the metallic clatter of his keys. The front door opened and shut, sealing me inside the warm, safe box he had built. I closed my eyes, finally letting go.

Chapter Twenty

A Safe Place to Break Down

I stared at the widening water stain on the plaster ceiling, the *drip-drip-drip* echoing like a mocking metronome in the empty bakery. My petite shoulders ached, a deep, bone-weary throb from hauling fifty-pound bags of flour. I just needed to survive the night. I had to prove I could do this alone.

For my entire life, the rule was simple: if I did not carry the weight, it crushed me. But as the freezing mountain wind rattled the shattered window frame, a treacherous, exhausting desire bloomed in my chest.

I wanted Grady.

The thought terrified me more than the failing plumbing. If I let myself crave his quiet confidence, if I let myself rely on those massive, scarred hands to hold my crumbling world together, what would happen to the fiercely independent woman I had built myself to be?

Yet, my soul ached to surrender. To just close my eyes and let him take the heavy tools from my blistered fingers. I was fighting so hard to keep my walls up, but God, I was drowning.

Above me, the ceiling gave a sickening crack, icy water rushing down toward my open recipe books. I squeezed my eyes shut.

Then, the rotted plaster completely failed.

A violent deluge of freezing, filthy water crashed over the prep table. It hit my shoulders like a physical blow, soaking instantly through my thin thermal shirt. The shock of the sub-zero cold punched the oxygen straight out of my lungs. I gasped, stumbling forward to grab my grandmother's leather-bound recipe book before the flood destroyed it entirely.

My boots slipped on the wet linoleum. I went down hard, my knees slamming violently into the floorboards. The icy water rained down on my hair, plastering wet blonde strands to my cheeks. I clutched the heavy book to my chest, my fingers completely numb. Freezing water pooled rapidly around my legs, spreading across the clean floor I had spent hours sweeping. The old iron pipe in the ceiling had ruptured completely, vomiting decades of rust and melted snow directly into my workspace.

I sat in the freezing puddle and sobbed.

The sound ripped from my throat, raw and ugly. I was not crying over the ruined plaster. I was weeping because the absolute, crushing weight of fighting the universe single-handedly finally broke my spine. I was freezing, alone, and entirely defeated. No matter how hard I worked, no matter how much ambition I poured into this mountain town, the building was actively rejecting me. I pulled my knees to my chest, burying my face in the wet leather of the notebook.

The deadbolt on the alley door ground open with a loud, metallic scrape.

The heavy steel door swung wide. A violent gust of snow blew into the utility corridor. Grady stepped through the threshold. He carried a massive, industrial Hobart planetary mixer against his chest as if the three-hundred-pound machine weighed absolutely nothing. Snow covered his dark hair and the broad expanse of his shoulders. Thick metal chains hung from his heavy leather toolbelt. The man was a walking fortress, completely impervious to the blizzard raging outside.

He kicked the door shut backward, sealing out the storm.

He turned toward the kitchen. He stopped dead.

His gaze dropped to the rushing water. He tracked the ruined plaster, the flooded linoleum, and finally landed directly on me. I huddled on the floorboards, soaking wet, hugging a ruined book, and shaking violently.

The massive Hobart mixer hit the dry section of the floorboards with a deafening *clang*.

He did not ask what happened. He did not hesitate. He moved with terrifying, immediate purpose. He crossed the kitchen in three long strides, bypassing me entirely to reach the utility closet. He reached up, his immense hand gripping the rusted main shut-off valve near the water heater. The metal shrieked. A sharp, brutal twist of his thick wrist, and the rushing water instantly stopped.

The sudden silence in the bakery was deafening, save for the erratic, jagged hitch of my breathing and the residual dripping from the ceiling.

Grady turned around. The fierce, territorial focus carved into his harsh features halted the frantic beating of my pulse. He ignored the ruined ceiling. He ignored the industrial machinery he had just hauled fifty miles through a blizzard. His entire world narrowed down to the freezing woman shivering on the floorboards.

He crossed the distance between us and dropped to his knees. The filthy water soaked instantly into his heavy denim jeans. He ignored the damage to his clothes.

"Drop the book." He reached for my icy hands.

"It is ruined." My teeth chattered so violently I could barely form the words. "The water—the floor is completely destroyed, Grady. I cannot afford—"

"Drop the book, Maisie." The command was low, a gravelly anchor leaving absolutely no room for debate.

My frozen fingers went slack. The leather-bound notebook hit the wet floor with a wet slap.

He grabbed my wrists. His calloused hands were a blazing furnace, radiating impossible heat. He pulled me forward, lifting me entirely out of the icy puddle. I collapsed against his broad chest. The thick flannel of his shirt absorbed the wet chill dripping from my hair. I wrapped my arms around his wide neck, burying my face into his shoulder. He smelled like cut pine, motor oil, and absolute safety.

He stood up, carrying my weight effortlessly. He did not set me down. He marched straight through the swinging door, up the creaking wooden stairs, and into the dark, quiet sanctuary of the apartment.

The woodstove radiated a thick, heavy heat in the corner, holding back the winter chill. He carried me to the bed and set me down gently on the edge of the mattress. The old metal springs groaned under the sudden shift.

"You are freezing." He knelt on the rug in front of me, his rough hands immediately gripping the hem of my soaked thermal shirt. "Arms up."

I lifted my arms. He pulled the freezing, wet fabric over my head and tossed it onto the floorboards. The cold air of the bedroom bit into my bare skin, forcing a violent shudder through my ribs. He worked faster. He unbuttoned my soaked jeans, peeling the heavy, wet denim down my legs and pulling off my ruined socks.

In less than thirty seconds, he stripped away every freezing, miserable layer of my failure.

I sat on the edge of the mattress, wearing absolutely nothing, my teeth clicking together. I crossed my arms over my chest. My racing pulse warred perfectly with the heavy safety of his massive presence.

He stood up. He unbuckled his heavy leather toolbelt. The thick rig hit the floorboards with a heavy thud. He stepped out of his wet boots and stripped off his water-logged jeans. He tossed his damp flannel shirt onto the chair. He stood before me in nothing but a pair of dark boxer briefs, the staggering width of his shoulders and the corded muscle of his abdomen glowing in the orange firelight.

He turned to the cedar dresser and grabbed a thick, dry thermal blanket.

He stepped right between my parted knees. He wrapped the heavy blanket entirely around my bare shoulders, gathering the ends tight beneath my chin. He trapped me in a protective cocoon of wool. Then, he sat on the edge of the mattress beside me. He hauled me sideways, pulling my blanket-wrapped body flush against his solid, hot side.

He wrapped his massive arms around me, burying his face into my cold, damp hair.

"I have you," he rumbled against my temple. The vibration of his voice sank directly into my bones. "You are completely safe. The water is off. The floor is fine."

"I was just trying to manage it." The confession scraped out of my throat. "The dripping started, and I thought I could put a bucket under it. I thought I could hold off the damage until morning."

"You do not have to hold off the damage." His thick hand stroked up and down my spine through the heavy blanket, generating a slow, steady friction. "I am the contractor. You are the baker. I fix the broken pipes. You stay warm."

"I cannot keep leaning on you like this." I turned my face into his hot neck. The scent of his skin grounded my spinning mind. "I am supposed to be capable, Grady. If I cannot even keep the ceiling from caving in, how am I supposed to run a successful business?"

He stopped rubbing my back. He pulled away just enough to look down at me. The pale scars on his jawline stood out against the harsh, uncompromising set of his features.

"Independence is a lie people tell themselves when they do not have anyone strong enough to catch them." His voice was heavy and absolute. "You fought alone because you had strictly no other choice. That former contractor robbed you. The world demanded you bleed for every inch. But that is over now. I am right here. I am never letting you fall."

The raw magnitude of his devotion broke the last stubborn lock on my heart. I did not want to fight him anymore. I did not want to prove my worth through suffering and isolation. I just wanted him.

I let the heavy thermal blanket slip off my shoulders. It pooled at my waist, leaving my upper body completely exposed to the warm air of the room.

Grady went perfectly still. A muscle feathered in his square jaw. His eyes tracked the gooseflesh rising on my arms, lingering heavily on the curve of my breasts. The protective, caretaking instinct radiating from him instantly shifted into a dark, consuming hunger. The equalizing shift settled perfectly into place. I was small, physically helpless against his strength, but right now, I held the absolute center of his world.

"Warm me up." I reached out, pressing my cold palms flat against the staggering width of his bare chest. The heat coming off his skin was a blazing furnace.

He answered with a low, territorial groan.

He caught my hips, hauling me fully onto his lap. I straddled his thick thighs, the blanket falling away completely. I wrapped my legs around his waist, anchoring myself to him. His massive, calloused hands gripped my waist. He possessed me with terrifying strength, yet the pressure of his rough fingers was obsessively gentle.

He pulled my mouth down to his.

The kiss was a branding iron. He drove his tongue past my lips, claiming every inch of my breath. The taste of dark coffee and unfiltered masculine heat short-circuited my brain. I tangled my fingers deep into his dark hair, holding him against me. He devoured the lingering cold from my system, replacing the icy chill with a heavy, throbbing ache low in my stomach.

He broke the kiss, dragging his mouth down my jawline to the sensitive skin of my neck. He scraped his teeth over my pulse. I arched my spine, offering him total access. The frantic, buzzing tension that usually defined my existence completely vanished. He dismantled my mental load with his mouth and his rough hands.

"You are so damn beautiful." He dropped the praise roughly against my collarbone.

He laid me back against the pillows. The woodframe shrieked in protest as he followed me down. He caged me beneath his massive frame, bracketing my head with his scarred hands. The staggering width of his shoulders blocked out the entire room. He was a mountain.

He slid his rough thumbs down the soft expanse of my stomach. The blistering friction of his heavy callouses against my delicate skin sent a reckless heat straight to my core. He parted my thighs, settling himself directly over my center.

I opened for him willingly, completely wrecked by the absolute certainty in his gaze.

"Tell me you trust me," he demanded, his voice a gravelly whisper.

"I trust you." I dragged my nails lightly down his wide back. "I trust you with everything."

He aligned his hips and pushed forward.

He filled me completely in one slow, uncompromising thrust. The stretch forced a high, sharp gasp right out of my throat. I squeezed my eyes shut, overwhelmed by the intense, absolute fullness of him. He froze, bracing his weight on his forearms, giving my body the time it needed to adjust to his staggering size.

"Look at me," he ordered softly.

I opened my eyes. He stared down at me with fierce, relentless worship.

"You take me so well," he praised, grinding his hips a fraction of an inch deeper. "Perfectly."

My lungs burned for air. I nodded, entirely unable to speak. The friction was a blazing fire, burning away the last remnants of the freezing water and the broken pipes.

He began to move. He set a slow, punishing rhythm, drawing almost completely out before driving deep again. The wooden bedframe slammed against the drywall. I wrapped my arms around his wide neck, clinging to him as he systematically took me apart. He anchored my hips with his large hands, adjusting the angle to hit the most sensitive bundle of nerves with every single thrust.

He did not rush. He worked my body with the exact same meticulous, obsessive focus he applied to building load-bearing walls. He mapped my reactions, learning exactly how to draw the loudest cries from my throat.

"Grady." The plea fractured as he ground deep.

"I am right here." He caught my mouth, swallowing my moans.

The tension coiled tight in my lower stomach. I rode the heavy, desperate impacts, entirely surrendering my control to the massive builder holding me down. He was pouring every ounce of his stamina into making sure I felt secure. The physical contrast fueled the fire inside me. His hands completely dwarfed my waist. His chest crushed the air from my lungs in the best possible way.

He picked up the pace. His hips snapped forward with uncompromising efficiency. Sweat beaded on his shoulders, dripping onto my flushed chest. The friction built into a blinding crescendo.

"Let it go," he demanded, his thumbs pressing hard into my hip bones. "Give it all to me."

My control violently snapped. The delicate muscles of my core clenched hard around him. I shattered, crying out his name as blinding waves of pleasure ripped through my bloodstream. He groaned, a deep, guttural sound that vibrated directly into my chest. He drove into me one final time, burying himself entirely to the hilt, and rode out his own powerful release.

The world outside the frosted glass dropped away completely.

He collapsed to the side, taking his crushing weight off my petite frame, but he refused to let me go. He hauled me flush against his side, tucking my head under his chin. He pulled the thick thermal blanket back over us, sealing in the deep, heavy heat of his body.

The erratic drumming of my pulse slowed as I rested my cheek against his bare chest. I listened to the steady, powerful thud of his heart. The storm outside continued to dump snow over the mountain town, but the frantic panic was gone.

"The mixer," I murmured sleepily, my fingers tracing a pale scar on his pectoral muscle.

"Is sitting safely downstairs in the dry half of the kitchen." He kissed the top of my head, his large hand smoothing down my back. "The plumbing is shut off. I will replace the broken pipe tomorrow morning. I already have the PVC and the joining compound in my truck."

I closed my eyes. I did not ask about the cost. I did not ask how long it would take. I just let the information settle into my brain, completely devoid of anxiety. He had handled it. He had fixed it before I even had to ask.

"Thank you," I whispered.

"Go to sleep, Maisie." His gravelly voice rumbled deep in his expansive chest. "I handle the heavy lifting."

Chapter Twenty-One

TORQUE AND TENSION

Maisie pushed a stray blonde curl out of her eyes. She pressed her flour-dusted palms flat against the gleaming butcher-block counter. Tomorrow morning, the heavy oak front door would unlock. The grand opening of a bakery she had poured her last dime and every shred of her sanity into. Cold, sharp panic fluttered beneath her ribs. If the croissants fell flat, if the mountain locals refused to show up, she stood to lose everything.

The custom ovens hummed a steady, perfect rhythm against the back wall. Grady had installed those heavy steel units with his own scarred hands. The low vibration rattled the floorboards under her boots. The terrifying, breathless vulnerability of no longer standing alone settled heavily in her throat. For ten exhausting years, independence acted as her only armor. She carried the weight of the world entirely by herself.

Then Grady ducked under her shattered doorframe. A mountain of a man in a heavy leather toolbelt. He systematically dismantled her defenses over the past month. He asked for absolutely nothing in return. He built subfloors, fixed burst pipes, and physically hauled her to bed when she collapsed over her recipe books.

A deep, desperate ache bloomed low in her stomach. She wanted to lean into him. She wanted to surrender to the quiet, unconditional safety of his broad shoulders forever. But accepting his sanctuary without guilt required success. She had to prove this bakery was worth the ground he worshipped.

She reached for her heavy wooden rolling pin.

Across the massive kitchen, the industrial Hobart mixer ground to life. The machine weighed three hundred pounds, and Grady had carried it through a blizzard just to keep her on schedule. He stood directly over the steel bowl. He tore open a fifty-pound sack of wholesale flour.

Maisie stopped rolling the pastry dough. She watched him work.

The temperature in the kitchen was pushing eighty degrees. Grady wore a tight, faded grey thermal shirt pushed up past his elbows. The thick veins in his massive forearms stood out like steel cables beneath his tanned, scarred skin. Every movement stretched the cotton tight across the staggering width of his chest. White flour dusted his dark hair and clung to his broad shoulders. His heavy, battered jeans hung low on his narrow hips, drawing her absolute focus down to the thick, corded muscle of his thighs. He was a machine built for brutal, unyielding labor. Yet the way his calloused, grease-stained hands meticulously measured out heavy pounds of sugar and butter made her core ache with a heavy, throbbing heat. The raw, unfiltered masculinity radiating off him short-circuited her brain. She wanted him to push her backward onto the stainless steel prep table, part her knees, and use every ounce of that relentless stamina directly on her.

He dumped the flour into the spinning bowl. He did not spill a single speck.

"Liquid ratios." His gravelly voice rumbled across the room, demanding her focus. "Give me the numbers, Maisie."

She blinked, shaking the inappropriate haze from her mind. "Four quarts of whole milk. Two dozen eggs. Keep the water ice-cold."

He nodded once. He reached into the commercial refrigerator. He pulled out the heavy gallon jugs with one hand.

They fell into a grueling, synchronized rhythm. There was no need for conversation. There were no arguments over process or technique. He respected her absolute authority over the recipes, operating as her physical extension. When she needed a massive block of cold butter broken down into cubes, he took the heavy chef's knife and hacked through the fat in seconds flat. When the brioche dough finished mixing, she did not even have to ask for help lifting the thirty-quart bowl.

Grady stepped up behind her. His chest brushed her spine. His massive hands clamped over the rim of the steel bowl, entirely dwarfing her own fingers. He hoisted the heavy metal off the machine, carrying it to the proofing racks without a single grunt of effort.

The scent of his cut pine and motor oil mixed perfectly with the sweet vanilla and yeast rising in the warm air.

By two in the morning, the physical toll of the prep work began to drag at her completely. Her wrists burned. The muscles in her lower back screamed in protest. She leaned over the butcher-block counter, trying to fold a massive sheet of laminated croissant dough. The butter block was too cold. The dough resisted the rolling pin.

Her hands began to shake. The ghost of her previous failures crept into her mind. The old contractor robbing her. The empty bank account. The terrifying prospect of the doors opening to an empty street. If she ruined this batch, she would run out of butter.

The rolling pin slipped. The dough tore.

"No." A ragged sound scraped out of her throat. She pressed her fingers over the tear, frantically trying to pinch the cold dough back together. The butter smeared across the wood. "No, no, no."

Heavy boots crossed the linoleum.

Grady stopped directly beside her. He did not attempt to fix the pastry himself. He knew his limits, and he respected her expertise entirely. Instead, he reached out and gripped her hips. His large, calloused hands anchored her shaking frame. The blistering heat pouring off his skin grounded her racing pulse.

"Step back," he commanded softly.

"It is tearing." Her voice cracked. "If the butter leaks out, the layers will not laminate. The entire batch is ruined, Grady. I do not have enough backup inventory to replace it."

He turned her gently around. He forced her to face his massive, solid chest. "Look at me."

She tipped her chin up. The pale scars tracking across his jawline caught the harsh overhead light.

"You are the best pastry chef in this state," he stated. The absolute certainty in his gravelly voice left zero room for debate. "You spent three days straight testing ratios for this exact temperature. You know the math. You know the science. Take a breath and fix it."

He did not offer empty platitudes. He did not tell her it was going to be fine. He directly reinforced her own competence. The equalizing shift in his respect acted like a shot of pure adrenaline directly into her veins. She was not a helpless victim anymore. She was the boss of this kitchen, and she had a titan standing at her back.

Her lungs burned for air. She drew in a sharp breath. "The dough needs to rest. Five minutes in the blast chiller to firm the butter back up."

"Done." He released her hips.

He scooped the heavy wooden cutting board entirely off the counter, carrying the massive sheet of ruined dough to the commercial freezer. He slid it onto the metal rack and slammed the heavy door shut.

The crisis averted, a sudden, heavy silence fell over the kitchen. The adrenaline spike left Maisie hollow and trembling. The dark night pressed against the newly installed, frosted windows. A terrifying thought struck her. If she succeeded tomorrow, if the bakery became profitable and self-sustaining, his job here would officially end. The broken pipes were fixed. The roof was secure. The heavy lifting was done.

What reason would he have to stay?

She stared at his broad back as he wiped down the steel prep tables. The prospect of operating this shop without his quiet, towering presence behind her tore a massive, devastating hole in her chest. She needed him. Not for his hammer, not for his truck, but for the fierce, unbroken devotion he poured into her every single day.

He turned around, tossing the damp rag onto the sink basin. He pinned her with a stare. He read the lingering panic in her expression with terrifying precision.

He closed the distance between them in two long strides. He stopped right in front of her, his massive frame blocking out the rest of the kitchen.

"What is going on in that head of yours?" he asked, his voice dropping an octave.

"The work is done." The confession slipped past her lips, raw and completely unguarded. "The building is finished, Grady. The machines are running. Tomorrow, we open."

"I know." He reached up, his rough thumbs sweeping a smudge of flour off her cheek. "You built a castle, Maisie. They are going to line up around the block."

"But what happens after?" She grabbed his thick wrists. Her small fingers could not even wrap halfway around his forearms. "You fixed everything. There are no more broken boards. There are no more flooded basements. What do you do when there is nothing left to repair?"

A dark amusement lit his harsh features. The muscle feathered in his square jaw. He slipped his hands completely out of her grip, moving them down to cup her face.

"I maintain the foundation." He dropped the words between them like heavy blocks of granite. "Did you actually think I was going to pack up my toolbelt and walk away?"

"You are a contractor." The protest was weak, entirely starved of conviction. "You move on to the next job."

"This is my job." He pressed his forehead against hers. The heat of his skin sank directly into her skull. "You are my job. I am going to stand right beside that register tomorrow, and I am going to watch you conquer this town. Then I am going to lock the doors, carry you upstairs, and worship you until you cannot remember your own name. I am never leaving."

The raw, unfiltered possession in his vow obliterated her remaining fears. The terrifying vulnerability of leaning on him vanished, replaced by an unbreakable, concrete security. She did not have to earn his presence. He was already permanently bolted to her floorboards.

She slid her hands up his chest, tangling her fingers deep into his dark hair. She pulled his mouth down to hers.

He met the kiss with territorial hunger. He parted her lips, his tongue sweeping inside to claim her breath. The taste of strong coffee and raw masculine heat flooded her senses. He stepped into her space, his heavy thighs pressing flush against hers, pinning her back against the butcher-block counter. He consumed her lingering anxiety entirely, offering nothing but absolute, immovable strength.

He broke the kiss slowly. His breathing rattled deep in his expansive chest.

"Get the dough out of the freezer," he commanded roughly, stepping back to give her room to operate. "We have a display case to fill."

The final four hours of the night passed in a blur of intense, unrelenting labor. They worked side-by-side. Grady manned the massive Hobart mixer, portioning out thirty pounds of heavy macaron batter. Maisie stood at the custom ovens, rotating heavy steel baking sheets. The heat in the room climbed steadily.

Zero arguments. Pure efficiency.

They loaded the massive oak display case at the front of the shop. Grady carried the heavy glass shelves from the back room, sliding them perfectly into the wooden brackets he had built last week. Maisie followed right behind him, arranging the food.

Hundreds of perfect pastries lined the glass. Golden, flaky croissants. Pastel pink and green macarons. Dozens of heavy, sugar-crusted brioche buns. The smell of yeast, toasted almonds, and burnt sugar soaked into the walls. The bakery looked exactly like the dream she had sketched on a napkin ten years ago.

Dawn broke over the mountains. The first rays of pale morning light hit the frosted windows, casting a soft glow over the gleaming wood floors.

Maisie stood behind the register. Her apron was completely ruined, caked in white powder and dried butter. Her arms trembled from the sheer physical exertion. The exhaustion was absolute, dragging her bones toward the floor.

Grady stood on the opposite side of the counter. He held a damp towel in his scarred hand. He wore a dusting of flour in his dark hair. The grey thermal shirt clung to his massive chest, perfectly soaked with sweat. He wiped down the last section of the customer counter, ensuring the wood gleamed perfectly in the morning light.

He tossed the rag aside. He looked at the loaded display cases. He looked at the polished floors. Then, he looked directly at her.

The pride radiating off his harsh features was a physical weight. He did not smile. He just stared at her with deep, unadulterated reverence.

He walked around the heavy oak counter. He did not ask for permission. He stooped down, hooking one massive arm under her knees and the other around her waist. He lifted her entirely off the floorboards.

Maisie gasped, dropping her head onto his wide shoulder. Her exhausted muscles surrendered entirely to his overpowering strength.

"The doors unlock in two hours," he rumbled against her temple. He carried her away from the register, marching straight toward the back office. "You are going to lie down on the cot. I am going to make you a bacon sandwich. You are not moving a single muscle until I say so."

"I need to print the receipt paper."

"I already loaded the register." He kicked the office door open with his heavy steel-toed boot.

"The coffee machines."

"Brewing." He set her down gently onto the thick blankets of the back room cot.

He stood over her. The man was a titan, entirely covered in the physical evidence of his devotion to her success. Flour in his hair. Grease on his knuckles.

"I handle the heavy lifting, Maisie." He reached down and unfastened the strings of her ruined apron. "Now eat."

Chapter Twenty-Two

The Engine Already Running

Grady stood in the shadows of the utility corridor. His scarred hands curled into white-knuckled fists against his heavy denim thighs. He watched Maisie.

Three hours remained until the heavy oak front door unlocked. The weight of the impending sunrise practically vibrated off her petite, flour-dusted frame. She stood at the stainless-steel prep table, a blonde hurricane of ambition, piping thick vanilla buttercream onto a massive tray of cinnamon rolls. Her movements possessed a fierce, terrifying focus. Her knuckles were bone white. A fine tremor shook her delicate wrists.

He wanted nothing more than to cross the gleaming hardwood floor he had laid for her, pry the plastic piping bag from her grip, and swallow all her stress whole.

His chest ached with a primal, consuming need to just handle it. He rebuilt the rotting roof. He installed the massive custom ovens. He rewired the entire electrical grid of the building. But standing here in the dim morning light, a brutal realization hit him. He could not fix the frantic pulse beating at the base of her throat with a hammer. A collapsed pipe was a structural math problem. The invisible pressure threatening to crush the woman he worshipped was an entirely different beast.

He was obsessed with her resilience. He was addicted to the stubborn, unyielding tilt of her chin. He did not just want to build her a bakery. He wanted to build her a fortress.

Maisie dropped the piping bag. It hit the metal table with a dull slap. She gripped the edge of the counter, her head bowing forward. Her breathing turned jagged, echoing loudly over the low hum of the commercial refrigerators.

Grady pushed off the doorframe. The heavy thud of his steel-toed boots announced his approach. He crossed the kitchen in three massive strides.

She did not look up. "The frosting is too stiff. The temperature in here dropped. I need to whip it again. If it tears the brioche, the presentation is ruined."

"The presentation is flawless." He stopped directly behind her. The staggering width of his chest shielded her back from the cold draft of the alley door.

"It is not." Her voice fractured, completely stripped of its usual authority. "I need to dump the batch. I need to start over."

She reached for the heavy steel mixing bowl.

Grady reached out, his thick, calloused fingers wrapping securely around her delicate wrists. He halted her movement entirely. The blistering heat from his skin sank directly into her trembling joints. He did not squeeze, but the iron grip offered zero room for negotiation.

"Let go of the bowl, Maisie." The low, gravelly command rumbled deep in his expansive chest.

"I have to fix it."

"You are done fixing." He pulled her hands away from the metal. He turned her around by her waist.

Dark circles bruised the soft skin beneath her eyes. Her apron was a battlefield of powdered sugar and dried butter. A manic, exhausting terror commanded her expression. She stared down the barrel of her own grand opening, and the fear of the mountain town rejecting her tore her apart from the inside out.

"They are not going to show up." The confession scraped out of her throat. She pressed her face perfectly flat against the center of his chest. "I spent every dime. You spent weeks of free labor. If that door unlocks and the street is empty, I take you down with me."

Grady anchored his hands on her hips. A muscle feathered in his square jaw. The absolute agony of her doubt cut a massive, devastating hole straight through his armor. He could pour concrete foundations in his sleep, but watching her break down over a financial ledger brought him to his knees.

"No one is going down." He smoothed his rough palms over the curve of her spine, pressing a heavy, grounding friction into the tight muscles of her back. "You built a masterpiece. You put the work in. Now you reap the reward."

"You do not know that." She gripped the thick cotton of his grey thermal shirt. "The weather is bad. The local diner already sells coffee. Why would they come here?"

"Because you are the boss." He tilted her chin up. He forced her to look directly at the pale, jagged scars crossing his jawline. "Because there is not a single contractor, logger, or mechanic in a fifty-mile radius who has not heard me bragging about this place for the last month. If the street is empty at seven o'clock, I will drive my truck through town and drag them here by their collars."

A fractured sound broke past her lips. It was not quite a sob, but the heavy pressure in her lungs finally gave way. She sagged against him. Her entire weight surrendered to his massive frame. He absorbed the burden effortlessly.

"You are shaking," he observed. His dark eyes tracked the violent tremor in her shoulders. "When was the last time you ate?"

Maisie blinked. Her brow furrowed. "I tested the almond paste yesterday afternoon."

"Sugar is not fuel." Grady scooped her up. He hooked one thick arm under her knees and the other around her waist, lifting her entirely off the floorboards.

"Grady, the display case—"

"Is fully stocked." He carried her away from the stainless-steel prep tables and marched straight toward the back office. "The ovens are off. The floors are swept. The engine is already running, Maisie. Now we take care of the driver."

He kicked the office door completely open. The small room was warm, heated by a heavy-duty space heater he had wired perfectly into the corner. A sturdy military-style cot sat against the drywall, covered in thick wool blankets. He set her down gently perfectly in the center of the mattress.

"Do not move." He pointed a grease-stained finger directly at her face.

She crossed her arms over her chest. She did not attempt to stand up. The fight drained thoroughly from her system, leaving behind a hollow, exhausted shell.

Grady turned around. He walked back into the kitchen, his boots heavy against the wood. He moved with strict, territorial efficiency. He grabbed a thick cast-iron skillet from his own camping gear stashed beneath the counter. He slapped it onto the small electric burner he used to brew his dark roast coffee. He twisted the plastic dial to high. The metal coil glowed a violent orange.

He pulled a package of thick-cut bacon from the commercial refrigerator. He ripped the plastic open and dropped four heavy slabs of meat directly onto the hot iron.

The dense, rich smell of smoking fat filled the air, cutting brutally through the overwhelming sweetness of vanilla and yeast. He cracked three farm-fresh eggs directly into the hot bacon grease. He did not bother searching for a spatula. He flipped the eggs with a quick, snapping motion of his thick wrist. He grabbed two thick slices of leftover brioche bread and dropped them directly onto the burner grates to toast.

He assembled the heavy breakfast sandwich in under four minutes. He grabbed a bottle of cold spring water from the bottom shelf.

He carried the heavy ceramic plate back into the narrow office.

Maisie sat perfectly still on the cot. Her knees were pulled tight to her chest. She stared blankly at the drywall, entirely lost in the terrifying prospect of a failed business. She was a woman used to carrying an entire world on her shoulders, completely paralyzed by the fear that her strength was finally running out.

Grady sat beside her. The old metal springs shrieked in protest under his staggering weight. The cot dipped drastically, sliding her flush against his solid thigh.

He pressed the cold water bottle into her hands. "Drink."

She unscrewed the plastic cap. She took a slow, obedient sip.

He lifted the heavy plate. "Open."

She looked at the massive bacon and egg sandwich. "I cannot stomach that." She shook her head. "My stomach is tied in knots."

"Your stomach is empty." He held the food closer to her mouth. Grease stained his calloused fingertips. "You are running on a brutal adrenaline crash. You need protein, and you need it right now. Eat."

The uncompromising authority in his gravelly voice left absolutely no room for argument. Maisie opened her mouth. She took a small bite.

The rich, salty flavor of the bacon and the heavy butter from the toasted brioche hit her system. Her eyes fluttered shut. A tiny spark of life returned to her exhausted features. She reached for the sandwich.

Grady pulled the plate back exactly one inch. "Hands down. I feed you."

She dropped her hands back to her lap, surrendering completely to his caretaking. He fed her the entire sandwich, bite by slow bite. He meticulously wiped a stray crumb from the corner of her soft lips with his rough thumb. He watched the pale, terrifying cast of exhaustion fade from her cheeks. The violent trembling inside her delicate frame ceased entirely. The heavy, greasy food operated like a perfectly placed structural beam, reinforcing her collapsing foundation.

He set the empty plate on the floorboards. He took the water bottle from her grip and placed it beside the dish.

He turned fully toward her. He wrapped his massive arms entirely around her waist, dragging her across the mattress until she sat directly on his lap. She threw her legs over his thick thighs, straddling him. She buried her face into the curve of his hot, thick neck.

The equalizing balance of power settled heavy in the small room. He possessed her entirely, controlling her physical health with absolute dominance, yet he operated specifically to amplify her strength. They were a single, unified machine.

"Thank you," she rasped against his skin. Her breath ghosted over his collarbone.

"You never have to thank me for keeping you standing." He bracketed her head with his scarred hands. He dragged his rough thumbs over her temples, rubbing slow, heavy circles into her hairline. He systematically pushed the lingering panic straight out of her skull. "I am the contractor. I maintain the property. You are the property."

"I am terrified." Her fingers dug into the heavy fabric of his shirt. "If nobody walks through that door, everything you built is for nothing."

He stopped rubbing her temples. A muscle ticked hard in his jaw. The raw vulnerability of her fear demanded absolute destruction. She was separating herself from him, building an emotional wall where she took the entirety of the blame for a hypothetical failure.

"You think I built those display cases for the town?" He gripped her chin, tilting her face up to meet his intense stare. "You think I hauled that commercial mixer through a blizzard because I care about the local economy?"

"You built them for the bakery."

"I built them for you." He pressed a hard, open-mouthed kiss directly over her pulse point. "I do not give a damn about the bakery, Maisie. I give a damn about the woman running it. If this building burns to the ground today, I will buy a new lot tomorrow and pour a fresh foundation. You are my permanent address. Do you understand me?"

Her lungs burned for air. A solitary tear spilled over her lashes, tracking through the fine layer of powdered sugar on her cheek. "You would do that?"

"I would tear a mountain down with my bare hands if you asked for a better view." He brushed the tear away with his rough knuckle. "But nobody is burning anything down today. You are going to walk out there, unlock that heavy door, and conquer this town. And I am going to stand right behind you."

The concrete certainty in his vow anchored her entirely. The frantic, buzzing terror evaporated. She nodded against his chest, her breathing finally evening out into a slow, steady rhythm.

Grady shifted his weight. He dropped his large hands from her face down to her waist. He gripped the strings of her ruined, flour-caked apron. He pulled the knot loose. The heavy canvas fell away, leaving her in a simple, tight long-sleeve shirt.

He lifted her off his lap, setting her gently onto the edge of the cot.

He stood up. The massive span of his shoulders blocked the overhead light. He reached into the small closet and pulled out a pristine, perfectly clean white apron. He had washed and ironed it himself three days ago, hanging it specifically for this exact moment.

He dropped to his knees on the hard floorboards directly in front of her. The physical submission of the act held devastating weight. The mountain of a man lowered himself entirely to serve her. He slipped the clean loop over her blonde head. He brought the crisp white strings around her narrow waist, pulling them snug and tying a perfect, secure knot against her lower back.

He did not stand up immediately. He rested his heavy, calloused hands flat against her soft thighs. He leaned forward, burying his face directly into her stomach. He inhaled the scent of vanilla, sugar, and pure, unfiltered woman.

"You take everything I give you," he praised roughly against her cotton shirt. "You take the pressure. You take the work. You take me exactly as I am."

Maisie dragged her hands through his dark hair. She held his head tightly against her body. The lingering panic was completely gone, replaced by a deep, throbbing ache of absolute devotion.

"I cannot do it without you," she whispered.

"You never have to." He kissed the center of her stomach. He stood up, towering over her once again. He offered his massive, grease-stained hand.

She placed her delicate fingers into his palm. He pulled her to her feet.

They walked out of the office together.

The main kitchen sat perfectly pristine. The stainless-steel tables gleamed under the harsh overhead lights. The massive Hobart mixer rested silently in the corner. The heavy air smelled of toasted almonds, rich butter, and fresh coffee. It was a temple built for a single purpose, and the altar was fully prepped.

They moved through the swinging wooden doors to the front of the shop.

The early morning light broke over the mountain peaks, casting a bright, cold glow through the frosted front windows. The display cases stretched across the room, loaded heavily with hundreds of perfect, golden pastries. The sight was an absolute triumph of her ambition and his structural support.

Grady stopped behind the heavy oak register counter. He pulled a clean rag from his back pocket and wiped a single, invisible speck of dust from the polished wood.

He looked toward the front door.

"Maisie." His gravelly voice broke the quiet silence.

She stepped up beside him. She followed his gaze.

Beyond the large glass panes, the town was waking up. The snow plow idled across the street. The driver, Mike, sat in the cab, holding a battered thermos. Behind the plow, a line of heavy boots and thick winter coats stretched completely down the block.

Dozens of locals stood in the freezing cold. Loggers in high-visibility vests. Mechanics with grease on their jeans. Families bundled in thick scarves. They stood in the heavy snow, waiting patiently in the freezing dawn.

They had not rejected her. They showed up exactly as Grady promised they would.

Maisie pressed her hand hard against her mouth. A ragged gasp tore from her throat. She looked up at Grady.

He did not smile. He simply stared down at her with fierce, unyielding pride. He reached out, his massive hand wrapping around the back of her neck in a heavy, protective hold. He squeezed gently, sending a blazing jolt of heat straight down her spine.

"The engine is running," he commanded softly. "Open the doors."

She nodded. She wiped her eyes, squared her small shoulders, and marched across the hardwood floor. She gripped the heavy brass deadbolt. She turned the metal lock with a loud, satisfying click.

She pulled the heavy oak door completely open.

The freezing mountain air rushed into the warm bakery, carrying the low hum of conversation and the crunch of boots on fresh snow. The crowd outside shifted forward, their eyes landing on the petite blonde baker and the massive, scarred contractor standing shoulder-to-shoulder behind the gleaming counter.

"Morning, Maisie." Mike stomped the snow off his boots on the front mat. He pulled a crumpled twenty-dollar bill from his insulated jacket. "Grady told us we would freeze to death if we didn't eat one of your cinnamon rolls today."

Grady stood like a stone wall behind the register, his arm's crossed over his expansive chest. He nodded once at the plow driver.

Maisie grabbed a pair of silver tongs. She turned toward the loaded display case. "I have them fresh out of the oven, Mike. How many do you need?"

Chapter Twenty-Three

FRESH PAINT AND A FULL HOUSE

The scent of vanilla and browned butter fills the warm air. I stare at the 'OPEN' sign resting against the newly polished mahogany counter. My heart hammers a frantic, terrifying rhythm against my ribs. Today is the day. For years, I carried the crushing weight of my ambitions entirely alone. I operated under the punishing law that if I did not break my own back, my dreams would shatter. Inheriting this crumbling mountain bakery was supposed to be my solitary, exhausting uphill battle.

Then Grady walked through the shattered doorframe.

I trace my trembling fingers over the gleaming pastry display case. The heavy glass panes sit perfectly inside the custom oak frames built by his scarred, calloused hands. The heavy, suffocating pressure gripping my chest is not just about whether customers walk through that door today. It is the raw terror of having let somebody help me. The bruised, fiercely independent part of my soul wars violently with a desperate, aching desire to finally surrender. Every sturdy wood beam above my head, every perfectly calibrated commercial oven, serves as a silent promise from a man who asks for absolutely nothing but the privilege of easing my burdens. I want this grand opening to succeed more than I need air to breathe. Looking around this flawless sanctuary he built, I just want to be worthy of him.

"It is seven o'clock," Grady rumbles. He steps up beside me. The staggering width of his chest blocks the draft from the utility corridor.

I grip the edge of the mahogany counter. "Turn the deadbolt."

He reaches past me. The heavy brass lock clicks loudly in the quiet room. He pulls the heavy oak door open.

A violent blast of freezing mountain air rushes into the warm shop. It carries the sharp scent of pine needles and heavy diesel exhaust. The quiet completely vanishes. The brass bell above the door rings.

Mike stomps his heavy, snow-covered boots on the front mat. The local plow driver marches directly to the register, pulling off his thick winter gloves. Behind him, a massive line of heavy winter coats stretches entirely down the icy block.

"Morning, Maisie." Mike drops a crisp fifty-dollar bill onto the polished wood. "Grady warned the entire dispatch office last night. He promised to personally tow our rigs into the ravine if we did not clear out your inventory by noon. Give me four cinnamon rolls and a dark roast."

"Coming right up." I grab a pair of silver tongs. A fine tremor shakes my wrist as I lift the massive, golden pastries from the glass case. I drop them perfectly into a white cardboard box. I fold the heavy tabs shut.

Grady stands at the commercial espresso machine. The heavy steel appliance looks like a toy next to his towering, muscular frame. He operates the steaming wand with brutal efficiency. His massive, scarred hands grip the delicate ceramic cup, totally dwarfing the white porcelain. A dark amusement lights his harsh features.

"I meant every word, Mike." Grady sets a steaming coffee on the pickup counter. "Drink up. Move your truck. You are blocking the crosswalk."

The plow driver laughs, grabbing his thick cardboard cup.

The brass bell rings continuously for the next three hours. A relentless tide of locals floods the bakery. Loggers wearing high-visibility vests cram into the small seating area. Mechanics with grease under their fingernails point at the pastel macarons in the display case. Exhaustion drags heavily at my bones. My lower back throbs from the repetitive motion of reaching across the wide counter. The heat of the ovens presses relentlessly against my spine.

The pastry case empties at a terrifying speed. The absolute panic I anticipated never arrives.

"I need the almond croissants," I call out over the loud hum of conversation. "The front tray is completely gone."

Grady abandons the coffee station entirely. He marches across the hardwood floor to the massive custom ovens he installed last week. He pulls a pair of thick, heavy leather work gloves from the back pocket of his denim jeans. He slides the rough cowhide over his massive hands. He rips the heavy oven door open. A blast of blistering heat rolls across the kitchen.

He grips the blazing-hot steel baking sheet, his flesh completely protected by the thick leather. He carries the heavy metal tray to the display case, sliding it perfectly onto the wooden racks. The heat radiates off the steel, cutting through the cold draft from the front window.

He pulls the heavy leather gloves off his hands. He tosses them onto the stainless steel prep table. He turns his fierce, territorial focus back to the coffee orders.

For ten agonizing years, I operated in a constant state of brutal survival. If I ran out of pan liners, I washed them myself until my knuckles bled. If a tray burned, I absorbed the financial loss and skipped meals to cover the deficit. I carried the crushing burden of my ambitions entirely alone, convinced that admitting I needed help meant weakness.

But the act of him anticipating the empty display case dismantles my defensive walls completely. He solves the logistical nightmare before the words even leave my mouth. The relief is a heavy, physical anchor dragging me down from the terrifying ledge of independence. I am not fighting a solitary war anymore. I am completely, utterly cared for. The profound intimacy of his relentless service rewrites the foundation of my soul.

The line snakes out the door and around the icy corner. Mr. Henderson, the local dairy supplier, steps up to the register. He pulls a leather wallet from his thick wool coat.

"I need two dozen of the brioche buns, Maisie." He points a gloved finger at the bottom shelf. "My wife refuses to make the Sunday roast without them. This place looks incredible. I heard the old contractor left you with a collapsed ceiling."

"He did." I punch the numbers into the point-of-sale tablet. "But I hired a better crew."

Mr. Henderson looks past me. He stares at the massive contractor wiping a spill off the coffee counter. "You hired the best man in the county. Nobody builds them stronger than Grady."

"I know." I hand him the heavy cardboard box.

We operate as a single, perfectly balanced machine. We are equals. He does not treat me like a fragile glass doll to be hidden away in the back room. He positions me exactly at the front of the battle, acting as my heavy artillery.

A tourist in a designer ski jacket steps to the front of the line. He ignores me completely. He leans over the mahogany counter to flag Grady down.

"Hey, buddy," the tourist barks. "Can you get me a black coffee and a dozen assorted pastries? Make it quick. I have to get to the slopes."

Grady stops packing espresso grounds. He rests his massive hands flat on the counter. He pins the man with a cold, unyielding stare.

"Talk to the boss." Grady points a thick finger directly at me. "She takes the orders. I pour the coffee. You wait your turn."

The tourist blinks, properly chastised. He turns to me and gives his order quietly.

By hour four, the physical demand of the morning rush violently attacks my nervous system. I grip the edge of the mahogany counter. Black spots dance in the corners of my vision. A dull ache throbs at the base of my skull.

A thick, calloused hand enters my peripheral vision.

Grady presses a cold plastic water bottle directly into my palm. The cap is already unscrewed.

I tip my chin up. He stands perfectly still beside me. The loud noise of the crowded bakery fades completely into the background. His dark eyes scan my flushed face. He reaches out, his rough thumb tracking over my jawline to wipe away a smear of powdered sugar.

"Drink," he commands softly.

I lift the plastic bottle. The cold water slides down my dry throat. The old contractor left me without running water for three agonizing days while I cried alone in the dark. Now, a mountain of a man hands me purified spring water without me ever having to ask. He anticipates the ache in my throat before my brain registers the discomfort. The brutal act of handing me a simple beverage shatters the impenetrable armor I wore for a decade. The relief is a massive, physical wave washing away the bitter sting of isolation. I do not have to monitor my own breaking point anymore. He is watching the gauges for me.

The afternoon sun breaks through the heavy winter clouds. Long, bright beams of light cut across the hardwood floor. The brass bell above the door finally goes silent.

I stare at the massive oak display cases.

They are completely empty. Not a single crumb remains. We sold four hundred pastries in less than six hours.

I rest my hands perfectly flat on the mahogany counter. My lungs burn for air. The terrifying prospect of failure, the agonizing nights spent crying over spreadsheets, the absolute dread of the town rejecting my food—it all vanishes. The air rushes out of me in a ragged, uneven exhale.

Grady walks to the front door. He grips the small rectangular sign hanging in the glass pane. He flips it over.

The red letters read: SOLD OUT.

He turns the heavy brass deadbolt, sealing us inside the warm, quiet sanctuary of the bakery.

He does not celebrate with a loud shout. He does not demand a victory lap. He walks past me, his heavy boots thudding against the wood, heading straight for the utility closet. He emerges a moment later carrying a heavy, industrial mop and a yellow bucket of hot, soapy water.

He drops the bucket onto the floorboards. He grips the long wooden handle. He begins to systematically clean the melted snow, rock salt, and mud dragged in by the massive crowd.

The thick muscles of his back shift beneath his tight grey thermal shirt. The staggering width of his shoulders moves in a steady, punishing rhythm. The wet cotton slides over the hardwood, leaving behind a gleaming, pristine surface.

He cleans my property. He scrubs the mud away, protecting the investment we built together. Every swipe of the heavy mop acts as a silent vow. The absolute intimacy of a massive, capable man doing the grueling, unglamorous labor just to preserve my energy wrecks me completely. He does not buy my affection with expensive gifts. He builds my security with his own two hands. He eliminates the mess so I never have to look at it.

I step out from behind the register. I walk across the damp floorboards.

Grady stops mopping. He leans his heavy weight against the wooden handle. He watches me approach. His chest rises and falls with slow, steady breaths.

"You missed a spot," I whisper. I stop inches from his solid chest.

A dark amusement lights his face. He abandons the mop entirely. The wooden handle clatters loudly against the drywall. He reaches out. His massive hands wrap securely around my waist. He lifts me directly off the floorboards, pulling my body flush against his hard torso.

"You conquered the mountain, Maisie." His gravelly voice rumbles deep in his chest.

"We conquered it." I wrap my arms tight around his wide neck. "I could not have baked a single loaf without the ovens. I could not have opened the doors without the floor. You built the foundation."

"And you built the empire." He tilts my chin up. "I handle the heavy lifting. You handle the rest."

He kisses me. The claim is absolute. The taste of dark roast coffee and raw masculine heat floods my senses. I open my mouth, taking his tongue, entirely surrendering my control to the massive contractor holding me completely off the ground. The lingering fear of independence drops away forever. I am exactly where I belong.

He breaks the kiss. He presses his forehead against mine. The quiet hum of the custom refrigerators fills the warm room.

"Go upstairs," he orders softly, setting me back down on my feet. "Take a hot shower. Get into bed."

"I have to clean the mixing bowls."

"I will clean the mixing bowls." He points a calloused finger toward the wooden staircase in the back. "I will wipe down the stainless steel. I will finish mopping the floor. I will lock the registers. You are off the clock."

"Grady—"

"Upstairs." The command is low, a gravelly anchor leaving zero room for debate. "I will be up in thirty minutes to worship the absolute hell out of you. Do not make me carry you."

The empty bakery sits perfectly quiet. The man who fixed my broken dreams stands in the center of the room.

"Thirty minutes," I agree.

I turn and walk toward the stairs. I leave the empty bakery, the dirty mixing bowls, and the heavy burden of consequence in the rough, calloused hands of the man who loves me. I do not look back. I know the foundation is secure.

Chapter Twenty-Four

Unloading the Truck Bed

The brass bell above the front door chimes one final time.

Mike, the local plow driver, steps out into the freezing mountain evening, carrying the very last white cardboard box of frosted cinnamon rolls. The heavy oak door clicks shut in his wake. The deadbolt slides into place with a sharp, metallic thud.

I stand behind the polished mahogany counter, staring at the empty room. A profound, ringing silence settles over the bakery.

The glass display cases sit completely bare. Only a few stray crumbs of toasted almond and a dusting of powdered sugar remain on the wooden shelves. Less than ten hours ago, those racks held over four hundred pastries. My hands grip the edge of the register. My knuckles stretch white beneath my skin. The brutal, gnawing terror that had chewed at my stomach for the last month dissolves into the warm, vanilla-scented air.

We sold out. Every single item.

The frantic, desperate survival mode that dictated my entire adult life begins to slowly power down. No ignored collection calls. No skipped meals to afford wholesale butter. I stare at the gleaming floorboards, the flawless custom ovens humming quietly in the back, and the sturdy structural beams overhead. The bakery is a triumph. The business is a success.

And I did not build it alone.

Grady steps out of the utility corridor. He carries a damp rag in his scarred fist. He tosses it onto the stainless steel prep station. He doesn't say a word about the empty cases or the stacks of cash secured in the drop safe. He just crosses the room, his steel-toed boots thudding against the wood, and stops mere inches from where I stand.

He reaches out, his rough thumb tracking over my jawline to wipe away a smudge of dried flour.

"The kitchen is locked down," he murmurs, his gravelly voice vibrating in the quiet space. "The ovens are off. Go upstairs."

"We need to prep the yeast for tomorrow morning." I blink, fighting the exhaustion dragging at my bones.

"I already fed the starter." He drops his hand, hooking his thick thumbs into the belt loops of his denim jeans. "You have been on your feet since two in the morning. Go take a hot shower. Wash the flour out of your hair."

I nod, too tired to argue with the sheer competence of the man. I untie the stiff, batter-stained canvas apron from my waist, leaving it draped over the back counter. I walk toward the rear wooden staircase, leaving him to finish wiping down the espresso machines.

My legs tremble as I climb the steps to the apartment.

The door clicks shut behind me. I move straight to the small bathroom, shedding my clothes onto the tile floor. I twist the shower handle, welcoming the blast of scalding water. The hot spray hits my shoulders, sluicing away the sweat, the flour, and the residual anxiety of the grand opening. I close my eyes, letting the steam fill my lungs. The physical relief is absolute.

Ten minutes later, I step out. The bathroom mirror is fogged over. I dry my skin with a thick towel, the rough cotton stimulating my exhausted nerves. I pull on a clean pair of simple black cotton underwear. I bypass my own neatly folded clothes in the bedroom and grab the faded charcoal-gray t-shirt Grady tossed over the armchair last night.

I pull the soft fabric over my head. It swallows my torso, the hem brushing my mid-thigh. The shirt smells like cut pine, motor oil, and his distinct brand of raw, unfiltered heat.

I walk barefoot into the small kitchen area and pour a glass of cold tap water. I lean against the formica counter, looking out the window at the snow-covered street. The town is dark now, illuminated only by the amber glow of the streetlamps.

The heavy tread of boots on the wooden stairs breaks the quiet.

The front door swings open. Grady steps inside.

He didn't come up empty-handed. My pulse spikes, sending a rush of heat straight down my spine. He stripped off his thermal shirt downstairs, wearing only a fitted, short-sleeved white undershirt that clings to his damp skin. Dust coats the broad expanse of his shoulders. Thick veins map the corded muscles of his forearms, pulsing with every flex of his large fingers against the steel handles of his toolboxes. The faded denim of his jeans rides low on his hips, hugging his thick thighs with a snug tension that leaves my mouth instantly dry. He is a walking, breathing monument to hard labor. The sheer masculine grit radiating from his large frame makes a reckless, pooling heat bloom low in my stomach. I want to drag my nails down his solid chest. I want those rough, calloused hands gripping my hips.

He sets the steel toolboxes down near the entryway. They land with a solid, definitive thud.

He turns back to the hallway. He retrieves a battered, dark leather duffel bag. He carries it inside, his broad shoulders passing effortlessly through the doorframe he reinforced just two weeks ago. He walks directly past the living room couch and drops the duffel bag in the corner of my bedroom.

I stare at the scarred leather from the kitchen.

Just a bag. But the visual strikes the foundation of my independence like a swung hammer. I spent my adult life building defensive walls, hoarding my pennies, trusting absolutely no one. Dependency was a dangerous luxury I could not afford. If a pipe burst in my old apartment, I panicked and taped it. If I let him stay, if I let him unpack those flannel shirts into my sparse closet, I surrender the isolation that kept me safe.

My throat tightens. The urge to flee wars with a desperate, aching need to finally rest. What if I forget how to survive alone? What if the fortress I built crumbles because I let a man carry the load?

Grady walks out of the bedroom. He stops in the center of the living area, wiping his dusty palms on his denim-clad thighs. He reads the sudden, rigid posture of my spine. He doesn't offer a hyperbolic declaration. He doesn't treat me like a fragile glass doll about to shatter.

"I counted the register," he says quietly. "You cleared a month's operating budget in a single shift. The bank deposit is ready for the morning."

"You brought your bags up." The words scrape past my lips.

"I did."

"Did your landlord hike the rent on your cabin?"

A dark amusement lights his harsh features. "I own the cabin, Maisie. It sits on ten acres of prime timber."

"Then why is your duffel bag sitting on my bedroom floor?"

He crosses the short distance between us in three long strides. He stops just inches from where I stand against the counter. The staggering width of his chest blocks the draft from the window. He boxes me in, but it isn't a cage. It is a shield.

"Because I do not live there anymore." The words are a low, gravelly rumble.

"You didn't ask."

"I am not asking." He lifts his scarred hands, resting them flat on the counter on either side of my hips. He leans in, the heat of his skin washing over my face. "I poured the concrete for the ovens. I wired the display cases. I watched you feed half the county today with your own two hands. You are the boss of this shop, Maisie. You do not need me to fix the roof anymore."

"No," I admit softly. "The roof is solid."

"The business is successful. The pipes hold water." He tilts his head, his dark gaze tracking the erratic flutter of my pulse at the base of my throat. "You survived. You won. Now, you get to build a life. And I am going to be the man standing beside you while you do it."

The cold, sharp blade of fear beneath my ribs vanishes. He isn't trying to rule me. He isn't offering charity to a broken girl. We are equals. I am the architect of this bakery, and he is the unyielding foundation holding the floorboards steady.

"I've never shared my space before," I confess, my fingers curling into the hem of his oversized shirt.

"I know." He lifts his right hand, tracking his rough knuckles down the side of my neck. "Which side of the closet is mine?"

"The left." The answer slips out effortlessly.

"Good." He slides his hands down to grip my waist. His thick fingers possess a terrifying strength, yet the pressure against my soft skin is obsessively gentle. "Where do you want my boots?"

"By the door."

"Done."

He lifts me directly off the linoleum floor.

A sharp gasp leaves my mouth. I wrap my arms tight around his wide neck, anchoring myself to him. He carries me out of the small kitchen, his chest a solid wall of muscle beneath my cheek. He bypasses the living room entirely, marching straight into the bedroom. He ignores the duffel bag resting in the corner.

He sets me down on the edge of the mattress. The bedsprings groan under the sudden shift in weight.

Grady doesn't join me on the bed. He drops to his knees on the hardwood floor right in front of me. The physical submission of the act holds devastating weight. The man who hauls three-hundred-pound steel mixers through blizzards lowers himself entirely to serve me.

He reaches out, grabbing my bare right ankle. He lifts my leg, resting my foot flat against his thick thigh.

"You stood for twelve hours," he murmurs, his dark eyes fixed on my face.

His massive thumbs dig into the arch of my foot. The pressure is blunt, exact, and agonizingly perfect. He kneads the stiff, cramped muscles with the meticulous focus of a craftsman seeking structural flaws. A long, satisfied groan hums in my throat. I drop my head back, my spine bowing against the headboard.

"Better?" he asks, moving his rough palms up to my calf.

"Much better." I look down at him. "You must be exhausted too. You carried the heavy flour sacks all morning."

"I am fine." He massages the tight muscle of my calf, his callouses creating a blazing friction against my skin. "I am built for the heavy lifting. You are built for the details. Together, the machine runs."

He sets my right foot down and lifts my left, repeating the slow, grueling massage. He works the tension out of my joints until my limbs feel like warm syrup. The sheer luxury of having a capable man tend to my physical pain overwrites a decade of lonely suffering. He doesn't buy me expensive spa days; he uses his own two hands to ensure I can walk tomorrow.

He finishes with my legs. He stands up, towering over the bed.

He reaches for the hem of his damp white undershirt. In one swift motion, he pulls the cotton over his head and tosses it onto the floorboards. The pale, jagged scars tracking across his ribs and collarbone catch the low light of the bedside lamp. He is rugged, imposing, and undeniably mine.

I reach out, pressing my palms flat against his washboard stomach. The heat burning beneath his skin is a furnace. I drag my nails lightly upward, mapping the hard lines of his chest. His breathing hitches. A muscle feathers in his square jaw.

"My turn," I whisper.

He doesn't hesitate. He steps between my parted knees. He grips the hem of the charcoal t-shirt I wear and pulls it up, drawing the soft fabric over my head. He tosses it aside, leaving me in nothing but my black underwear.

The cool air of the room kisses my bare skin, but the intense, territorial heat radiating from his gaze immediately warms my blood.

He pushes me back onto the mattress. The wood frame shrieks as he follows me down, caging my smaller body beneath his immense frame. He braces his weight on his forearms, ensuring he doesn't crush me, while his broad shoulders effectively block out the rest of the room.

"You are so damn beautiful," he praises roughly, his voice dropping an octave.

He buries his face in the curve of my neck. His scruff scrapes delightfully against my sensitive skin. He drags his open mouth over my collarbone, scraping his teeth lightly over my pulse. I arch my back, offering him total access. The buzzing tension that used to define my existence is completely gone, replaced by a heavy, throbbing ache low in my stomach.

I tangle my fingers deep into his dark hair, holding him against me. "Grady."

"I am right here." He drops the vow against my skin.

He slides his calloused hand down my stomach, the rough texture of his palm sending a violent shiver of anticipation through my core. He hooks his fingers under the elastic band of my underwear and pulls them smoothly down my hips, tossing the fabric off the edge of the bed.

He parts my thighs, settling himself directly over my center.

I open for him willingly, entirely wrecked by the absolute certainty in his posture. He reaches between us, his rough thumb finding the swollen, sensitive bundle of nerves. He presses down, applying firm, deliberate friction.

A ragged gasp tears out of my throat. My hips buck up off the sheets.

"Look at me," he commands softly.

I force my eyes open. He stares down at me with fierce, relentless worship.

He guides himself to my entrance. He pushes forward, filling me in one slow, uncompromising thrust. The stretch forces a tight, desperate sound from my lips. I squeeze my eyes shut, overwhelmed by the intense fullness of him. He freezes, bracing his weight, giving my body the time it needs to adjust to his staggering size.

"You take me so well," he murmurs, his voice a gravelly whisper against my ear. "Exactly what I need."

My lungs burn for air. I nod, unable to form a coherent sentence.

He sets a slow, punishing rhythm. He draws almost completely out before driving deep again. The wooden bedframe slams rhythmically against the drywall. I wrap my arms around his wide back, my nails digging half-moons into his scarred skin. He anchors my hips with his large hands, adjusting the angle to hit the absolute deepest point of friction with every single thrust.

He maps my reactions. Every time a fractured moan escapes my lips, he grinds his hips a fraction of an inch deeper, exploiting the vulnerability. He works my body with the same meticulous, obsessive focus he applies to his trade.

"Maisie," he groans, a deep, guttural sound that vibrates directly into my chest.

The tension coils tight in my lower stomach. I ride the desperate impacts, surrendering my control to the massive builder holding me down. The physical contrast fuels the blazing fire inside me. His hands dwarf my waist. His chest crushes the air from my lungs in the best possible way. We are moving as a unit, completely synchronized.

Sweat beads on his forehead, dripping onto my flushed chest. He picks up the pace. His hips snap forward with unyielding efficiency.

"Let go," he demands, his thumbs pressing hard into my hip bones. "Give it to me."

My control violently snaps. The delicate muscles of my core clench hard around him. I shatter into a blinding climax, crying out his name as waves of pure pleasure rip through my bloodstream. He drives into me one final time, burying himself to the hilt, and rides out his own powerful release with a harsh, ragged shout.

The world outside the frosted windows drops away.

He collapses to the side, taking his crushing weight off my frame, but he refuses to let me go. He hauls me flush against his side, tucking my head under his chin. He reaches down and pulls the thick duvet up over our bare shoulders, sealing in the deep, heavy heat of his body.

The erratic drumming of my pulse slows as I rest my cheek against his chest. I listen to the steady, powerful thud of his heart.

The room is dark. The bakery downstairs is locked and secure. The duffel bag sits quietly in the corner, a promise rather than a threat.

"Tomorrow," Grady murmurs sleepily, his large hand smoothing down my bare back, "I am going to build a new set of shelves for the pantry. The wholesale delivery is coming on Tuesday. You need the space."

I trace a pale scar on his pectoral muscle. I don't ask about the cost of the lumber. I don't worry about the time it will take. I just let the information settle into my brain, completely devoid of anxiety. He handles the structural integrity. I handle the recipes.

"Okay," I whisper.

He kisses the top of my head, holding me tight against his side. The lone survivor is dead. The partnership has officially begun.

Chapter Twenty-Five

EVERYTHING IN WORKING ORDER

The ambient heat of the custom ovens wrapped around my shoulders like a thick blanket. Tuesday mornings belonged entirely to prep work and inventory. I sat on a solid maple stool at the stainless-steel counter, staring down at the glowing screen of my tablet. The spreadsheet numbers glowed in absolute, undeniable black. No red deficits. No panicked calculations about which utility bill to float for another two weeks.

For my entire life, my greatest survival mechanism had been an absolute refusal to lean on anyone. Carrying the burdens of my ambition on my own petite shoulders was not just a habit; it was my armor. When I first inherited this crumbling mountain bakery, my deepest fear had not been the rotting floorboards or the shattered plumbing. It had been the terrifying vulnerability of needing help. I operated under the brutal assumption that dependency equaled destruction.

Then Grady walked through my shattered front door. An imposing mountain of a man with a thick leather toolbelt and quiet, steady eyes.

Now, listening to the flawless, rhythmic hum of the commercial refrigerators he wired with his own scarred hands, the last lingering remnants of my panic dissolved completely.

I looked across the flour-dusted kitchen. Grady stood near the utility sink, adjusting the water pressure valve with a steel wrench. His broad shoulders stretched the seams of his faded gray thermal shirt. The dense muscles of his forearms flexed precisely as he torqued the metal fitting.

For the first three months, I secretly waited for the other shoe to drop. I stayed awake at night, terrified his unconditional support came with a hidden invoice. I thought eventually he would demand control, or resent the grueling labor, or ask for a return on his immense investment.

Instead, he only ever wanted *me*.

The overwhelming desire to finally surrender washed through my veins, sweet and warm as vanilla sugar. I did not have to fight the universe alone anymore. Grady built me a sanctuary, not just out of drywall and copper piping, but out of absolute safety.

The sharp hiss of air brakes echoed from the back alley. The Tuesday wholesale delivery.

"I have the dock," Grady rumbled, tucking the wrench into his back pocket. "Stay seated."

"I need to check the inventory manifest." I slid off the maple stool.

He did not argue. He simply opened the reinforced steel back door, letting the crisp mountain air flood the corridor. We stepped out onto the concrete loading dock together.

The delivery driver, a new kid from the regional supplier, hopped out of the cab holding a clipboard. He looked at the towering contractor, then down at me.

"Forty bags of high-gluten flour," the driver announced, holding out the pen. "And twenty cases of unsalted butter."

"Let me see the invoice." I took the clipboard. Scanning the printed lines, a hard knot formed in my stomach. It was not panic. It was pure irritation. "You shorted us on the European butter. This lists domestic. I specifically ordered the high-fat content for the lamination process."

The driver scratched the back of his neck. "Warehouse must have swapped it. It bakes the same, lady."

"It absolutely does not bake the same." I tapped the pen against the plastic board. "I am not signing for this. Put the domestic butter back on the truck. Have dispatch hot-shot the correct European cases up the mountain by tomorrow morning, or I will pull my entire account and go to your competitor."

The driver blinked, clearly unaccustomed to the uncompromising demand. He looked toward Grady, seeking male solidarity or a softer negotiation.

Grady leaned his substantial weight against the brick wall, crossing his thick arms over his chest. A dark amusement lit his harsh features. "Do not look at me, kid. The boss gave you an order. Better get on the radio."

The driver swallowed hard, nodded, and scrambled back into the cab to fetch his dispatch radio.

Grady pushed off the brick. He stepped up right beside me, resting his calloused hand flat against the small of my back. The blistering heat of his palm seeped through my cotton shirt, anchoring me to the concrete.

"You tore him apart," Grady praised, his gravelly voice dropping to a rough whisper. "Flawless."

"He tried to compromise the croissants." I handed the clipboard back to the driver as he returned with a nervous apology and a promise for a rush delivery tomorrow.

"Nobody compromises your empire." Grady stepped away. He approached the open back of the truck, grabbing the first stack of hundred-pound flour sacks.

He hauled the immense weight effortlessly, stacking the dense paper bags onto a hand truck. We moved back inside. I directed the placement while he provided the raw physical power. We operated as a unified front.

The new pantry was a masterpiece of carpentry. Floor-to-ceiling wooden racks lined the walls, built from solid oak planks thick enough to hold an engine block. Grady slid the final sack of flour into its designated slot. He kicked the hand truck out into the hallway.

I checked off the final inventory box on my tablet. "We are fully stocked for the weekend."

Grady turned around. Closing the pantry door behind us, he shut out the humming noise of the kitchen. The small, enclosed space smelled intensely of raw pine and dried lavender.

He stepped into my space, his thighs boxing me against the lower storage rack. Reaching down, he plucked the tablet from my grip and tossed it onto a nearby shelf. He framed my face with his rough, grease-stained hands.

"Everything in working order?" he asked quietly, his thumbs brushing over my cheekbones.

"Perfectly secure." I slid my hands up his chest, tangling my fingers into the collar of his shirt.

He tilted his head and kissed me. The contact was completely devoid of the desperate, frantic energy of our early weeks. This was a deep, territorial claim. A slow burn of absolute certainty. He swept his tongue past my lips, tasting of dark roast coffee and masculine grit. I melted against his solid frame, entirely supported by the unyielding width of his chest.

"I swapped the bearings on the commercial mixer," he murmured against my mouth, breaking the kiss just enough to speak. "It spins quieter now. You will not get a headache during the morning prep."

"You anticipate everything." I rested my forehead against his chin.

"I maintain the foundation." He pressed a hard kiss to the crown of my head. "Come on. The yeast is blooming."

*

Epilogue

Eight months later.

The mountain town transformed into a pristine, silent world of white. Fat, wet snowflakes drifted past the frosted glass of the bakery's front windows, burying the sidewalks under a foot of fresh powder.

I stood behind the polished mahogany register, watching the snow fall. The 'CLOSED' sign hung on the door. The display cases were completely wiped out, scrubbed clean after another sold-out Sunday morning rush.

A dull ache throbbed in the base of my spine. I pressed my palm against the pronounced, round curve of my swollen stomach. At seven months pregnant, the grueling physical demands of the kitchen proved entirely exhausting. I shifted my stance, trying to relieve the pressure on my lower back.

A custom-built, padded stool slid effortlessly behind my knees.

I sat down with a grateful sigh, sinking into the thick leather cushion. Grady had constructed the chair three months ago, perfectly calibrating the height to the register counter so I never had to stand longer than necessary.

I turned my head. A plate of perfectly baked chocolate chip cookies rested on the stainless-steel prep table. I had spent the last hour working on a simple, comforting recipe rather than the complex French pastries that built our reputation. The rich smell of browned butter and melted chocolate saturated the warm air.

I picked up the ceramic plate. Carrying the warm treats toward the back of the building, I walked slowly over the polished floorboards.

The bakery footprint had expanded over the summer. We bought the vacant lot directly behind the shop, pouring a fresh concrete slab. Half of the new addition served as bulk ingredient storage, while the other half belonged entirely to Grady. It was his sanctuary—a fully equipped woodworking and maintenance shop.

I pushed the heavy steel door open with my shoulder.

The sharp scent of cut oak and wood glue greeted me, cutting through the sweetness of the cookies. The shop hummed with the low vibration of a space heater. Hand tools lined an imposing pegboard wall in perfect, meticulous order.

Grady stood in the center of the room at his sturdy workbench.

He wore a faded charcoal t-shirt, completely dusted in a fine layer of sawdust. The short sleeves gripped the thick, corded muscles of his biceps. Grasping a sanding block in his scarred right hand, he worked it smoothly along the curved stile of a wooden crib.

He moved with a punishing, obsessive focus. Dragging his bare left palm over the sanded wood, he checked the grain for the slightest imperfection. He refused to use metal screws or cheap brackets. He constructed the baby crib using traditional mortise and tenon joints, binding the solid oak with structural wood glue and dowels. He was building our child a bed designed to survive a century.

I leaned against the doorjamb, entirely captivated by the rugged display of competence.

"You are going to sand right through the wood," I teased softly.

Grady stopped. Dropping the sanding block onto the bench, he turned around. His dark gaze immediately dropped to my rounded stomach before rising to meet my eyes. The harsh, stoic lines of his face softened into an expression of pure, unadulterated reverence.

He grabbed a clean shop towel from his back pocket, wiping the thick layer of sawdust from his calloused palms. He crossed the concrete floor in three long strides.

"You are supposed to be resting on the couch upstairs." He stopped directly in front of me, his physical presence radiating a blistering heat.

"I baked." I held up the ceramic plate. "You shovelled the front walk three times today. You needed calories."

He reached out, his rough fingers wrapping gently around my wrist. Pulling my hand forward, he bent his head to take a bite directly from the warm cookie I held. He chewed slowly, his eyes never leaving mine.

"Incredible," he praised, his gravelly voice echoing in the quiet shop.

"It is just a basic recipe."

"Nothing you touch is basic." Taking the plate from my grip, he set it carefully onto a nearby tool cart.

He dropped to his knees on the concrete floor. The physical submission of the act still carried a devastating weight, even after all these months. The man who hauled industrial steel beams down the mountain lowered himself entirely to worship his family.

He pressed his large, warm hands against either side of my pregnant belly. His thumbs stroked slow, comforting circles over my tight shirt. Turning his head, he pressed a lingering, open-mouthed kiss directly to the center of my stomach.

The baby kicked in immediate response to the pressure.

A dark amusement lit Grady's face. He rested his cheek against the curve of my belly, absorbing the tiny, muffled impacts. "Strong," he murmured. "Building a sturdy foundation."

"She is kicking my ribs to pieces." I ran my fingers through his dark, dust-coated hair.

Grady stood back up, towering over me. Wrapping his thick arms entirely around my waist, he pulled my back flush against his broad chest. He anchored me, taking the strain completely off my aching spine. I melted into his solid frame, resting my head against his collarbone.

We looked at the half-finished oak crib sitting on the workbench.

"The joints are curing," he explained quietly, his deep voice vibrating into my shoulder blades. "I will apply the beeswax sealant tomorrow. It will be completely dry and set up in the nursery by the weekend."

I traced the pale, jagged scar crossing the back of his right hand. "You do not have to finish it so fast. We still have two months."

"I do not leave things unfinished, Maisie." Tightening his hold on me, he rested his chin securely on the top of my blonde head. "I make sure everything is ready before you ever have to ask."

The raw, unfiltered truth of his statement settled deep into my bones. He spent the last eight months proving that exact vow every single day. He changed the oil in my delivery van. He stocked the firewood. He rubbed the cramps out of my swollen feet until I fell asleep against his chest. He eradicated the terrifying isolation that once dictated my existence, replacing it with an unbreakable, concrete security.

I turned in his arms. I tipped my chin up, refusing to look away from his intense stare.

"I love you," I whispered.

He bracketed my jaw with his rough hands, his thumbs tracing the line of my cheekbones. "You are my life, Maisie. My permanent address."

He tilted his head and captured my lips. The kiss was slow, rich, and utterly devoted. The taste of warm chocolate and rugged masculine grit blended perfectly. Sliding my arms around his wide neck, I held him tightly against me. There were no walls left between us. No hidden fears of abandonment. He was bolted directly to my soul.

He broke the kiss gently, pressing his forehead against mine. His chest rose and fell in a steady, calming rhythm.

"Perfect," he murmured, his breath ghosting over my skin.

I leaned back against his substantial warmth, looking out the small workshop window. The snow outside continued to fall, completely burying the tight-knit town in white. Inside, the ovens hummed, the wood glue cured, and the foundation held entirely strong.

www.ingramcontent.com/pod-product-compliance
Lightning Source LLC
LaVergne TN
LVHW030921080826
845145LV00013B/2993

9781969650987